The last thing \
in Seattle's Pike Place Market and the strange woman. Had she been kidnapped? If whoever was responsible thought they could ransom her, wow, were they in for a surprise when no one came to her rescue.

She had nothing, less than nothing. She didn't even own a cat. How pathetic. If she vanished, there wasn't a cavalry on the way. All the scary movies she and her mom had watched rushed back. Few ended well.

She opened her eyes to half-mast and ventured a glance around the room. The sun streaming through the window wasn't as bright as before, as though it was now shrouded in clouds. Hardwood floors, and dark wood paneling. No pictures on the walls. Vanessa opened her eyes wider and moved her head to get a better view and locate the door.

A man sat in a rocking chair and stared at her without blinking. She couldn't turn away as though she were a doe who'd just realized a hunter had her in his sights. His long-sleeved shirt and his pants were leather, and his hazel eyes had flecks of gold and brown. Straight black hair flowed past broad shoulders, with a single thin warrior braid. A soldier of some sort was her first impression. His predatory gaze never wavered, as though assessing her as she had assessed her surroundings. She wasn't afraid, and that surprised her. She should be afraid. She should be terrified.

Praise for Pam Binder

"Pam Binder gracefully weaves elements of humor, magic and romantic tension."

~Publishers Weekly

~*~

"Ms. Binder establishes herself as a powerful and inventive voice in paranormal romance."

~Romantic Times

~*~

"Between the covers, you'll find not only a hero, a heroine, and the villain found in most romances, but a truly delightful and heartwarming romance."

~America Online Romance Fiction Forum

~*~

"Action-packed and filled with romance and danger."

~ParaNormal Romance Reviews

Wylder Times

by

Pam Binder

The Wylder West

Wylder Times

Cover Art by *The Wild Rose Press, Inc.*

The Wild Rose Press, Inc.
PO Box 708
Adams Basin, NY 14410-0708
Visit us at www.thewildrosepress.com

Publishing History
First Edition, 2022
Trade Paperback ISBN 978-1-5092-4284-9
Digital ISBN 978-1-5092-4285-6

The Wylder West
Published in the United States of America

Dedication

To my editor Nancy Swanson,
for her encouragement and dedication
to helping make my stories come alive

Chapter One

Douglas Eagle Greyeyes had failed.

It was not the first time the shapeshifter had lost sight of the creature who hunted him. His enemy was a proven adversary, with unlimited abilities to track his prey. But this was the first time his enemy had come this close. Greyeyes must stay vigilant. After the massacre, he'd brought what remained of his tribe, his aging and ill mother and younger sister, as far west as he dared. Unlike his enemy, Greyeyes' magic was connected to the mountains, and he believed their strength would protect his family. But his enemy must have found a way around the magic.

He would not underestimate his enemy again, or how deep ran his desire for revenge.

Greyeyes transformed from Thunderbird to man and settled on the topmost snowy peak of the jagged mountain range. Like the tips of spears, its pinnacles pierced through clouds as though to make war with the sky gods. From his vantage point, the world of man lay out before him in serene calm. But the closer to earth, the more the view changed. The pace was too fast for his liking. Humans rushed to build cities, to explore new lands, and even to love.

He had loved once when he was mated. A love he thought would last until he drew his last breath, as his kind mated for life. Their union was fated to end almost as soon as it had begun. A month after their wedding day, his enemy had attacked with his hordes, killing all in their path. He, his mother, and his sister had been gone that day, searching out a gift for his wife. They returned to a village in ash and ruin.

He knew he would never love again. Everything changed when the war between him and his enemy erupted. There was no time for mating or believing in a peaceful world. There was only survival.

If he were alone and not tied to the earth, by honor and duty, he would remain in the snow-covered world that touched the stars.

The sky darkened as the sun relinquished its duties and released the day to the moon.

It was time for him to check on his mother and sister.

With a deep sigh, and a prayer of thanks to the sky gods, Greyeyes leapt from the mountain peak and dove toward the earth. Wind rushed past him as he spread his arms and transformed into a Thunderbird.

Chapter Two

The smells greeted him first, and then the sound of his ten-year-old sister's laughter. His sister's name was Fala, and it meant crow. He had wondered at the choosing of such a name, but his mother had a way with the meaning of names, and the child had grown into her name with ease and grace, befriending not only crows, but all creatures that came into her orbit.

Greyeyes opened the door, presenting his gift. He'd seen the abandoned kitten when he landed from the sky and knew his sister would give it a good home.

Fala squealed and rushed toward him, dark hair braided, eyes wide, and arms spread like wings to accept the little furball. "For me?"

He smiled, grateful he had thought to bring her the kitten. "It asked for you by name. It had heard of your good heart."

One arm scooped the kitten up while the other reached out to hug him. "You tease. Kittens don't speak. At least ones this young."

"And who told you that?"

He heard his mother as she entered the room. Her step was more uncertain these days, and she shuffled, unsteady on her feet, her breathing more labored. He knew the signs. They all did. She was failing and running out of time.

His mother's face was as dark and lined as a

walnut, but the smile that crossed her face was ageless and full of love. "I told Fala that creatures speak to those with an open heart. Wash up for dinner. I've made your favorite."

"Everything you make is my favorite," Greyeyes said.

"I have raised a good son." She smiled. "Fala, please take your new kitten into your room and introduce her to the others."

Fala cradled the kitten in her arms and kissed her on the top of the head. "Do you think Midnight and Forest will like her? She is so little. It will be a long time before she can play with them."

His mother scratched the kitten behind the ear gently. "Your wolves will love her as much as you do, because you have raised them since they were as young as your new kitten and taught them to be gentle and kind. Now run along."

When Fala disappeared into her room, his mother motioned for Greyeyes to join her by the table. He sat opposite her, waiting for her words of wisdom. Before they were forced to flee their homeland, his mother was a respected and high-ranking wise woman and healer in their village. She was next in line to his father, the chief.

She searched his eyes, as she did more and more these days. "As you are aware, our enemy, Rammon, has found us."

His mother's announcement did not take Greyeyes by surprise. He'd learned as a child that his mother possessed extraordinary abilities. She never talked about them or named them. He'd asked her once about what magic she could claim as her own, and her answer was simply, "I can call on whatever I need."

"Our enemy is close, and yes, I believe he has found us, or at least our general direction. We can leave."

"The time for our leaving has passed. You must stand."

Greyeyes twisted the Thunderbird ring on his finger. "I respect your wisdom, but I fear I must question it this time. Fala is too young, and her training as a warrior not equal to what could face her if we confront our enemy." He did not include his mother and his worry about her frail condition. She knew her limitations better than he. Greyeyes didn't need to insult her by pointing it out to her.

"I agree, son. Fala is not ready. It saddens me to have you carry this burden. I would have spared you if I could. I will take Fala to a safe location. But I am not leaving you alone. I'm preparing to summon your mate."

Greyeyes straightened. "My mate was murdered by our enemy. I will have no other."

"The fates and the gods will give you another path. I have foreseen this in the stars."

A dark cloud settled around him as he remembered his village turned to ash. He and his wife had made plans for their future, named the children they would have, and counted their blessings that their marriage, although arranged, had evolved into a love match. "I doubt your prophecy. My kind only mates once. I had my chance at love."

His mother settled a shawl made from scraps of multi-colored cloth around her shoulders. "Your wife's death was five years ago, and she would want you to join the world of the living."

His anger rose. "You do not know what my wife would wish."

She heaved a sigh. "I know that she had loved you since you were children and would want you happy. This fight you face cannot be faced alone, and it will take a mated pair to defeat your enemy."

He laughed without humor. "Have you forgotten that I can only mate with another of my kind and all of those have been murdered? There is no one."

She reached out to hold both his hands in hers. "That is not true. There is someone. A woman of another time and place, with extraordinary gifts and strength."

"You give hope where there is none."

"I offer only truth and possibilities."

He drew away and rose to add more wood to the dying fire in the hearth. He was not prepared to mate, but if it meant the survival of his species… "You speak in riddles. Speak plain. Who is this woman who is to be my mate, and why did you not speak of her sooner? She must be summoned at once."

His mother sat back. "It is complicated."

He stirred the fire until it roared to life. "Again with the riddles. How is it complicated? The only way to defeat our enemy is if I confront him with my mate."

"The woman must agree to be your mate."

"If she knew the danger we faced, why wouldn't she want to help? What aren't you telling me?"

She drew her shawl around her. "When I consulted the stars for your mate, they answered, but at first the message was confusing. I didn't recognize the position of the stars until I realized that your mate is not from this time but a time in the distant future."

"I still do not understand the problem. We are star-walkers. We can travel to different times. You have told me that you have done so numerous times."

She nodded. "Yes, I have, and that is why it is complicated. The women from the time where your mate lives are not like the women you have known. They are independent, with minds of their own, and she might not agree to be your mate. You will have to woo her."

"You are joking."

"I am most serious. You must be on your best behavior at all times."

He narrowed his gaze. "What are you afraid to say?"

"She must not know that you are a shifter. It will be enough for her to grasp just knowing she has time traveled from her century to ours."

"You want me to hide who I am?"

His mother smiled for the first time. "Exactly." She stood. "I am taking Fala with me on the star-walk to the future. She will be safe there."

Greyeyes caught the hesitancy in his mother's voice. Her words were brave, but they both knew that nowhere was safe if their enemy lived. "How will I know this woman when she appears?"

"Trust your heart."

Chapter Three

Present Day

Pike Place Market stood between Seattle's downtown and the salt waters of the Puget Sound, an inlet to the Pacific Ocean and part of the Salish Sea. The market stood as a gateway between the city and the endless expanse of the Pacific Ocean.

Or at least that was how Vanessa O'Casey's mother had described the market when they first moved to Seattle ten years ago from Ireland. Vanessa loved the area immediately. She loved the closeness to the snowcapped mountains and being surrounded by lakes and the healing powers of the salt sea of Puget Sound.

That same day her mother had said that after twelve moves in as many years, they had finally found a place they could call home.

Vanessa had doubted her mother's words. Her mother had said the same thing every time they moved to a new city. Except this time, her mother had celebrated the move by buying them matching silver butterfly pendants. Her mother said butterflies symbolized transformation and hope and the courage to embrace a change that would make life better.

Vanessa had dismissed her mother's words and only half listened. Her mother was always saying new-age-y stuff like that. Vanessa touched the pendant her mother had given her. Even though its eyes were the same emerald-green shade as Vanessa's, she hadn't liked the gift. The butterfly stood for things she didn't think were possible.

The road in front of the market rolled and bucked beneath Vanessa's feet as an earthquake tremor reminded the city that Mother Nature was not in a good mood today. Vanessa yanked her suitcase over the curb. As a sales representative for a local glassblower, her suitcase contained samples, as well as a schedule of appointments. It was her first day, and she was determined this job would stick. Instead of jeans and a sweater, she'd worn her best navy-blue dress, with its matching suit jacket. She was determined to make a good impression.

She rolled toward the passageway that led to the craft booths selling everything from local honey, cheese, wood carvings and handblown glass, to the long stretch of flower venders. She reached the heart of the market where men tossed salmon into the air to the cheers of the crowd. The vendors showed the small tremors respect and secured their wares, but tourists either screamed in fear or giggled in delight. The vendors and screamers were the smart ones.

A few vendors waved or shouted her name as she passed. They were like her family, and over the years she'd worked for many of them, performing odd jobs when her mother first died and helping sell their crafts to tourists as she grew older. The man throwing the fish in the air winked at her as she passed.

She nodded, keeping her head down. A few weeks ago, he'd asked her to marry him, and she'd sidestepped his proposal by telling his fortune and predicting that he'd meet his true love before the next full moon. She should have told him she wasn't interested. She should have told them all no, outright, but she didn't want to hurt their feelings.

Love was a delicate thing.

Five years ago, when she'd turned twenty-one, men began flocking to her like bees to honey. At first, she dismissed it as a coincidence. She was no beauty, but men seemed drawn to her large green eyes and exotic features. Her mother had been an Irish Gypsy who told fortunes, and Vanessa used the ploy that although she wasn't interested in them, she'd vow to find them their soulmates. And she had. But love was not in the cards for Vanessa.

She was never going to fall in love.

Vanessa had made that vow to her mother as she lay dying on the rain-soaked street, covered in blood and tears. Vanessa had had two regrets that night. The first was not seeing the car in time as it sped in her mother's direction, and the second was not having the presence of mind to find her mother's pendant. It had disappeared when her mother was run over.

Vanessa's chest tightened as she picked up her suitcase and headed down a winding staircase to the next level of shops that meandered like a rabbit warren below the upper levels. Reaching the bottom, she tugged the suitcase over a crack in the concrete floor and heard something inside break.

"Perfect."

She was going to lose this job before she had a chance to start. But finding a job had never been the hard part. Staying employed was the challenge. She'd had a series of odd jobs that ranged from waitress, nanny, hotel maid, and even a custodian at an apartment complex she'd lived at over the summer. She either messed it up or became bored. Usually both happened simultaneously. Her mother had had the same issues and blamed it on their gypsy heritage. Whatever the reason, it was annoying. Her mother might have loved to wander the globe, but Vanessa hated it. Her dream was to settle in one place and put down deep roots.

Vanessa opened the double doors that led to the shops and moved to the side to inspect the individually wrapped handblown ornaments. Her fingers scraped on a shard of glass, and she flinched. The tip of a star ornament had broken off.

During her interview, the glassblower had said that Vanessa was responsible for the samples and would pay for anything she broke. Great. She hadn't been on the job a full day, and already she owed her employer money.

The glassblower had also given her instructions to tell the potential customer that he'd invented a new shade of blue that he called Space Glass. To Vanessa, it looked black and lifeless, like her life. Swell, she was in a pity party, and it wasn't even noon.

A tour group rushed past, and Vanessa spun to avoid them, lost her balance, and the ornament fell to the ground and shattered. She stared at the broken pieces until her eyes blurred.

A middle-aged woman, wearing a multicolored ankle-length dress that reminded Vanessa of a sunset, bent to place the broken ornament pieces in a basket. "Let me help you, Vanessa. I have just the thing to make this as right as rain."

"How do you know my name?"

The woman stood and motioned for Vanessa to follow her. "My name is Enola. Come. I want to show you something."

The woman led Vanessa to her shop. She motioned again for Vanessa to take a seat on an overstuffed green velvet sofa at a far wall, while she went to a counter where she placed the basket containing the shards of glass and covered them with a silk cloth.

There was a smell to the shop that Vanessa couldn't quite place, odd spices she couldn't identify mingled with cinnamon and nutmeg, as though someone had pulled a sweet bread from the oven. But that was silly. There weren't any restaurants on this level.

The small room was an eclectic blend of new and old, with rock-salt lamps, tarot cards, vintage collectables, and miniature replicas of the Space Needle. The shop's best feature was that it had a bird's-eye view of Puget Sound and the ferry terminal. In a corner by the window, a child around ten or eleven, with dark braids and dressed in jeans and an orange sweatshirt with the image of an Orca whale leaping out of the water, sat drawing with a blue-colored pencil.

The child glanced up when Vanessa entered. "I can't get the color of the water right, and I want my whale to feel at home."

Vanessa, loving that the child thought of the whale's feelings and the color of the ocean, said, "I was like you when I was your age. I wanted to make sure the water looked as good on paper as it did in my imagination or in real life. There was an old woman who lived near us in Ireland who gave me great advice. She said the water reflects not only the sky but the mood in the artist's heart. What colors do you think the whale would love to swim in today?"

The little girl's eyes lit up in a smile. "Our favorite colors are lavender."

"A beautiful choice. Add shades of lavender to the water, and a touch in the sky."

"Thank you." The little girl jumped down from her perch on the stool, gave Vanessa a quick hug, then jumped back on her perch and resumed her drawing.

Vanessa took in a breath as she turned from the child. She hadn't thought about the woman who'd given her that advice in a very long time.

"That was kind of you," Enola said, as she glanced up from the basket of broken glass.

Vanessa nodded. "I was just passing on a kindness. Your shop is brand new. I was here yesterday, and this space was empty. How did you move in so fast?"

"Magic," Enola said.

Vanessa started to laugh, but Enola was so serious, Vanessa cleared her throat instead. "Thank you again."

Her mother used to talk about magic in that same matter-of-fact tone. There would be times when Vanessa would misplace a slipper or her favorite rag doll, only to have her mother find it easily. When asked, the only response her mother would give would be to say, it was easy to find misplaced things when a person was magic.

What was happening to her? Today was full of memories she had fought to bury. Looking for a distraction, Vanessa examined a stack of old newspapers on a table. The papers were aged to a rich patina shade of sun-kissed gold. One was open to the want-ad section, and someone had circled an ad for an assistant in a watchmaker's shop.

Assistant for the town's watchmaker needed immediately.

Must be able to read, write, and like birds.

She laughed at the reference to birds. Very strange qualification for a watchmaker's assistant.

"Is something amusing, dear?"

Vanessa flipped the paper closed and read the location of the town and the date on the newspaper— Wylder, Wyoming, 1878. "The ad in this newspaper just seemed a bit odd, but I'm sure the owner of the watch shop had his reasons."

"There are reasons for everything. Sometimes, though, we can't see them clearly."

Vanessa nodded. "My mother would say the same kind of thing when I complained that I couldn't see the bottom of a lake. She told me I had to look deeper."

Vanessa glanced at the paper again before turning back to the woman. People always said there was a reason for everything. She hated that phrase. What was the reason that a hit-and-run driver had killed her mother? The police never found the driver and blamed it on rain and slick roads, and that a light had gone out on the corner where the accident occurred. The case was dismissed, and Vanessa had been assigned to live with foster parents.

But Vanessa was her mother's daughter, and she knew how to change her appearance and disappear. Living on the streets wasn't so bad when you knew how to survive. She and her mother had been doing it all their lives.

The woman reached for the basket and brought it over to Vanessa. "I fixed your ornament."

Vanessa lifted the cloth. The glass star was indeed in one piece. "How did you do that?"

"Do you believe in magic?"

"Who are you?"

"If I told you, I doubt you'd believe me."

The girl by the window put down her pencils. "You have to tell her, Mama. He doesn't have much time left. This is our last chance."

"Shush, dear heart. We've talked about this before. We must be patient. It is very important we send the right person."

"But shouldn't my brother be the one to make the decision?"

The grandfather clock in the shop chimed out the hour, echoing through Vanessa. She was late for her appointment with the shop owner a few doors down. She picked up the repaired ornament, marveling that it looked as good as new. "Thank you so much for repairing my ornament. How much do I owe you?"

The woman turned toward Vanessa. "Consider it a gift. Do you like birds?"

Vanessa held the ornament in both hands, reviewing the odd question, remembering it was also noted in the strange ad. "That was one of the qualifications in the ad."

"Indeed," the woman said.

"My brother likes birds," the child by the window said. "Do you?"

The clock chimed again. "I suppose so. I've never thought about it much. I suppose if they keep to themselves, I'm okay with them. I really need to go. I'm late."

"Mama. Do something. You can't let this one go."

The girl jumped down from her stool by the window. "Please, Mama. I like this one."

Okay, that wasn't creepy at all, Vanessa thought as she backed toward the door. She reached out behind her and turned the doorknob.

It was locked.

Chapter Four

Greyeyes ventured out of his watch shop as though pulled by an invisible cord. Stars covered the velvet sky over the western town of Wylder, with the moon hidden behind the clouds as though afraid to show its face. The evening was crisp and cold, with a promise of a storm in the air, which kept people snuggled in their homes for the night.

He knew all the constellations, first out of a child's curiosity and then out of survival. He knew their names, and legends, from the earliest of cultures to modern times. The Big Dipper—or Seven Brothers, in Blackfoot—shone in the sky, along with Wolf Trail—or as it was better known, the Milky Way—spreading its path across the sky. The familiar constellations usually brought comfort and stability to his thoughts. Not tonight. Tonight, their color tarnished as though covered by a thin veil.

And then he saw it, the constellation he always hoped he wouldn't find. They were difficult to locate unless you knew where to look. The French astronomer Nicolas Louis de Lacaille had first named the cluster Horologium in the eighteenth century, and the Latin name translated meant the Pendulum Clock. People believed there weren't any legends associated with the stars. Those people would be mistaken.

And then he heard it.

A loud clap in the sky, as though the pendulum clock had begun its countdown, brought the curious townsfolk to the windows. A herd of escaping cattle raced through the street, afraid, disoriented.

The second clap of lightning and thunder plunged the night into inky blackness and sent the few townsfolk still left outdoors fleeing into their homes and locking their doors.

A third clap and burst of light sent Greyeyes running for the center of the street, thankful the storm drove people from their windows. A short time ago a farmer had been struck by lightning while working his fields and died where he stood. The cause of the bolt from the sky took wings, veering from the natural to a supernatural origin in record time. The theories varied depending on the ancestry of the town's inhabitants. Those from Scandinavian descent, half joking, floated the idea that the bolt was sent down by the ancient god Thor. Some said it showed God's displeasure. Others that their town was cursed and that a great evil approached.

The last theory was closest to the truth.

Greyeyes reached the center of the street. A young woman, clad in clothes that had been torn to ribbons, lay covered by darkness and magic and foreboding. A thin veil of silver light sparkled around her as though protecting her from view. But as he approached, the veil seemed to let out a sigh of relief and then dissipate into the air like morning mist confronted by the warming rays of the sun.

He knew who had sent her and why she was here. He had been expecting her. But the sudden appearance of a woman would be difficult to explain. A naked woman—impossible. He had worked out the explanation, but he would have to get her inside before she was seen.

He scooped her into his arms and carried her to his clock shop, kicking the door open. A lone oil lamp cast long fingerlike shadows along the walls and lit his way to the back rooms. The woman's breathing was shallow, her long dark hair damp, her features pinched, and her eyes squeezed shut. He registered that she had been afraid when the star-spell had been cast. Had she known what to expect?

Would his mother have told the woman the reason for her journey, or kept it from her for fear she would say no?

The answer screamed as though spoken—the woman had been caught off guard.

Greyeyes gently set the woman on his bed beneath the window, covered her with a warm quilt, and stepped back. He settled in a rocking chair to watch over her. What remained of her clothes told him that she was not from around here. He had traveled the globe and lived longer than most of his kind. He was certain her clothes were not from this century, or from the one that had gone before. That left the possibility that his mother's search had taken her into the future.

But how far?

If that were the case, when the woman awoke how would she react? She would be disoriented, that was a given. But would she scream...try to run from him? Neither would matter.

From the window, a winter breeze seemed to move the stars from their positions. They shimmered and then, regaining their hold on the sky, cast their sights on the woman on the bed. Their light settled on a pendant half hidden under the blanket. Even hidden, the image was unmistakable. A butterfly, made from a polished silver metal, lay on the woman's chest.

Had his mother known about the pendant, what it symbolized and his goals for a better future for his people? It could be a coincidence the woman wore this symbol. But he didn't believe in coincidences, and neither did his mother.

But it made his decision easier.

He would explain the situation to the woman when she awoke, and what was expected of her. He hoped his mother had chosen well. If not, he would have to send the woman back to her own time. Failing to return the woman to whence she came from, he would have no other choice than to kill her.

The latter choice did not sit well, but if Rammon learned of the woman's existence, he would use her to wipe out what remained of Greyeyes' family.

He stretched out his legs and leaned back against the wood slats of the rocking chair. It would be a long night.

Chapter Five

Vanessa's eyes fluttered open, then closed against the glare of a morning sun streaming through a window. Even that small effort drew pain. Every muscle in her body ached as though she'd been tossed like wet clothes into the dryer. And she was so tired.

She was lying on a bed that felt crunchy, covered with a blanket that smelled like straw and dust and sweat. She scrunched her nose, but assessing her situation was more important than focusing on the hideous smell.

The last thing she remembered was the shop in Seattle's Pike Place Market and the strange woman. Had she been kidnapped? If whoever was responsible thought they could ransom her, wow, were they in for a surprise when no one came to her rescue.

She had nothing, less than nothing. She didn't even own a cat. How pathetic. If she vanished, there wasn't a cavalry on the way. All the scary movies she and her mom had watched rushed back. Few ended well.

She opened her eyes to half-mast and ventured a glance around the room. The sun streaming through the window wasn't as bright as before, as though it was now shrouded in clouds. Hardwood floors, and dark wood paneling. No pictures on the walls. Vanessa opened her eyes wider and moved her head to get a better view and locate the door.

A man sat in a rocking chair and stared at her without blinking. She couldn't turn away as though she were a doe who'd just realized a hunter had her in his sights. His long-sleeved shirt and his pants were leather, and his hazel eyes had flecks of gold and brown. Straight black hair flowed past broad shoulders, with a single thin warrior braid. A soldier of some sort was her first impression. His predatory gaze never wavered, as though assessing her as she had assessed her surroundings. She wasn't afraid, and that surprised her. She should be afraid. She should be terrified.

Lifting her chin, she stared back at him as though in challenge. Her mother had taught her how to defend herself, and she'd had to use those skills on more than one occasion. But she had no delusions that he could overpower her. And yet she kept her focus.

He leaned forward as his gaze roamed over her body, resting on her breasts. She glanced down and let out a strangled cry. Her clothes were shredded. She grabbed the blanket and pulled it up.

His expression, although predatory, had turned very male when he'd viewed her near nakedness. His behavior was like a slap in the face. Her mother had taught her how to deal with men like him.

She jutted out her chin and raised her voice. "Release me at once, or I'm calling the police."

An eyebrow arched, and the man tilted his head as though she were a strange species of woman he'd never seen before.

His reaction further stoked her anger. How dare she be treated like this? The first thing she was going to do, when she got out of this place, was report this man and the woman who'd kidnapped her to the authorities. She had no idea how the small child fit into the mix, but she'd bet her last box of cookies that the child was an innocent.

Vanessa gathered the thin blanket around her and slid to the floor. Her toes curled. The floor was so cold it hurt. She fought against the cold and marched toward the door. "I'm leaving, and you can't stop me."

He blocked the entrance. "I believe that I can."

She lifted the blanket, drew back, and kneed him in the groin. A startled expression covered his face. He winced and doubled over, groaning. She seized the moment, shoved him aside, and pulled the door open.

She raced through what appeared to be a watch shop and headed toward the exit. She was grabbed from behind and yanked around.

The man's face was easy to read. There was an equal balance of pain, humiliation, and surprise. "I told you not to leave."

"You said no such thing, you Neanderthal. I said you can't stop me, and you said you believed you could. I have a photographic memory, so I know what I said, and it hasn't changed. You can't stop me."

He released her and stood back, folding his arms across his chest. "Fine. Leave."

"I will." She nodded her head and regretted the action immediately. Her head throbbed as though she'd bashed it against a wall. In the back of her mind, her thoughts screamed that she had no clue where she was. Added to her growing fear, the man had given up too easily. Why?

But she couldn't think about that now. She had to get out of here before he changed his mind. The man was crazy strong. This wasn't the first time she'd had to knee a guy to prevent him from attacking, but in the past, they'd given up after she fought back. Her mother seemed to attract the wrong kind of men and joked that it was good her daughter was around to set the men straight.

She ignored the nagging thought that there was something she was missing and opened the door of the shop. She expected the watch shop to be in Pike Place Market, perhaps next to the strange woman's shop on the lower level. And if not, it was on the top level with the crowds, where traffic crept past searching for parking, where the flower stalls were, and men throwing salmon.

She pulled the blanket around her as her mouth gaped open. A wagon covered by a tarp and drawn by a team of tired horses plodded down the dirt road. The driver was hunched over the reins and tipped his hat to her as he drove past. Across the street were wooden buildings that looked like they had been yanked out of an old Wild West movie. In the distance, she heard gun shots. Someone yelled. A dog barked.

She stepped back.

"I thought you wanted to leave?" It was the man with the hazel eyes.

Her heart hammered in her chest. "Where am I?"

"A better question would be 'when am I.' To save time, I'll answer both. You are in Wylder, Wyoming, eighteen hundred and seventy-eight."

Chapter Six

The woman fainted into his arms.

No surprise. Traveling through time put a strain on the body, and it was not unusual for people to sleep for days after the event and awaken with a pounding headache.

Greyeyes carried her back inside and propped her on a chair in the front of the shop. He ruled out placing her in his bed. From her reaction when she'd awoken, she'd misunderstood his intentions. He wouldn't make that mistake again. Obviously, his mother hadn't informed the woman of the reason for her journey.

Frustrated, he felt a muscle over his temple throb. This lack of information would make it more difficult for her.

He lit an oil lamp and set it beside the chair. The light highlighted the fire in her dark hair, and the long lashes that fanned over pale, almost translucent skin. She was bone thin and had felt as light as feathers in his arms. How could this frail woman help him when Rammon arrived? The thought was ludicrous. His mother must have made a mistake. He needed a warrior beside him, not a damsel in distress.

He frowned, remembering how she had attacked him when she woke. There had been no fear in her eyes, only rage. Her attack had taken him by surprise, and he was never surprised. Her delicate appearance and her first response were a contradiction. She was braver than she appeared. He pulled his eyebrows together and raised the blanket over her bare shoulder. What was he going to do with her?

There was no telling how long she would be unconscious. He stoked the fire in the woodburning stove in the kitchen at the end of the hall, and set the kettle on the burner to heat water for coffee. He'd spend the night catching up on his reading. He needed to keep his mind off the problem that was slumped over in the chair in his shop. He'd felt surprised when his mother had first proposed the idea of searching for someone to help him defeat his enemy. He hadn't stopped her at first. He didn't believe she would be successful, and second, and more importantly, it had served the purpose of getting both her and his sister to safety.

He pulled a chair opposite the woman and opened the stack of newspapers he'd collected, letting his mind travel from one article to the next. When he'd finished one, he reached for another.

He'd taken a break to find clothes for the woman to wear, from an assortment that belonged to his mother and sister, and placed them over a chair in the kitchen. When finished with the task he'd settled once again to read and take notes. Somewhere in the articles was bound to be a hint of the forces that were moving toward Wylder. There was always a trail if you knew where to look.

Time passed, and soon the night was finished and welcoming the early rays of the morning sun.

The woman's eyelashes fluttered and rose over eyes the color of green grass after a spring rain.

She sat up straighter, clutching the blanket to her as

she scanned the shop. She took in great gulps of air and cleared her throat. "Did you say that I've traveled to the year eighteen hundred and seventy-eight?"

He set the newspaper aside. Hours had passed, and yet she had clung to this question as though it had occurred to her only minutes ago. "Yes, you have traveled to the past." He was fearful to say more. There would be time later. Then he amended the thought. It might already be too late.

She shook her head. "Be serious. I'm not in the mood for jokes. Where am I? A Hollywood movie set? An elaborate Wild West reenactment convention? Wait. I know. I heard of this place in Washington State where they preserved the town exactly the way it was when it was first built in the eighteen eighties. I think it was called Winthrop."

He kept his voice low so as to not spook her. She reminded him of a deer cornered by a predator. He didn't like the comparison, as he knew very well that she viewed him as the hunter, and for some reason that bothered him.

"I don't know of this place you call Winthrop. This is Wylder, eighteen seventy-eight, and there is a simple explanation."

"Simple?" Her voice was strong, but her knuckles shone white as she clutched the blanket tighter, belying her fear. "You tell me I have traveled back in time, and I'm supposed to believe there's a simple explanation? Either I'm dreaming…"

"This is not a dream."

"Or," she said through clenched teeth, "you are a crazy person." She took a deep, ragged breath.

He leaned toward her, trying to figure out where to

27

start. In his world, all of what he was about to say made sense, but he knew, from experience, that others thought of what he was about to explain as more magic and myth and legend than reality.

"I'm not crazy. I'm part of a tribe of Star-Walkers, which means we can travel places by using the star constellations. My mother and sister set out on a journey to find someone who would become my partner." He paused, deciding to keep the need for the quest, and the consequences if they failed, to himself. "They obviously traveled to your time and then sent you back to me."

Her lips pinched together. "Partner? As in wife?" Her frown deepened. "The answer is a hard no."

He shook his head. "I don't need a wife."

The words he spoke rang false. He might not need a wife, but he needed someone. But how was she part of this?

"Please. Let me go."

Her plea tore at his heart. She was an innocent thrown into his path. It was clear his mother had made a mistake, and despite his earlier vow to kill her, he knew that was not an option. But neither was sending her back, at least not yet. He rose and crossed over to the hearth where he had a kettle of coffee. He touched the side of the kettle. Still warm. "Would you like a cup of coffee?" He turned. "Do they drink coffee in your time?"

Her nod was slow. "We call them lattés, and I like mine with chocolate syrup, caramel, and cream."

Odd request, from an even odder woman. To classify her as different from anyone he had ever met was an understatement. "I don't have any of those

ingredients. They might have them at the store."
Greyeyes reached for two tin cups that hung from
wooden pegs. He filled the cups and handed her one.

She wrapped her hands around the cup, took a sip,
and frowned. "This is the worst coffee I have ever
tasted." She gazed at him over the rim of the cup. "Any
chance you have clothes I could wear? Or do you like
your women in rags?"

He winced. She didn't fear him and said whatever
was on her mind. "I set clothes aside for you in the
kitchen."

"Good." She stood, snatching the blanket around
her body. "Point me in the direction of the kitchen, and
if you're thinking of helping me dress, think again."

He pointed to the back of the shop. "I'll show you
the way."

She held up her hand. "Don't bother." Her head
held high, she turned in a flourish, the blanket and
tattered clothes swirling around her like the robe of a
queen.

He watched her leave. She was brazen and
confident, he'd give her that much. But he'd fought
beside confident warriors before and watched them be
cut down in the prime of their lives and die. What he
faced, what they both would face if she was the one,
would take more than confidence. It would take that
unknown quality of a person's character that was only
apparent when they faced the enemy.

And if they failed? Failure was not an option.

Too many lives depended on defeating his enemy.

Chapter Seven

Vanessa shut the door of the kitchen and leaned against it, gathering strength from the solid wood. Her whole body shook. She had to escape this crazy person. She scanned the room. A woodburning stove gave off waves of heat. An oil-burning lamp stood in the center of a wood table, and over the chairs was an assortment of dresses and petticoats that had seen better days.

Petticoats?

Had she really used that word? But that's the only way to describe the frilly skirts draped over the chairs.

Okay. Get a grip. Mr. Tall, Dark, and Delusional had claimed she had traveled back into the Wild West, and obviously he was determined to keep that theme alive. All she had to do was escape, get to a phone, and call 9-1-1. Easy, peasy.

She stripped out of what used to be her best business dress and jacket, and what remained of her undergarments, and reached for a gray petticoat she thought may have been white once. From what she had seen, it was freezing outside, so she decided to put on as many layers as she could. She found boots and slipped them on, surprised they fit.

"Do you need any help?"

She snapped her attention toward the door. Would he barge in? She needed an escape plan. She searched the room and grabbed a cast-iron skillet, slid a chair to the side of the closed door, and stood on the chair.

"Yes," she said, lowering her voice to a breathy, come-hither tone. "Can you help me?" She pressed her lips together and held the skillet like a baseball bat.

The door opened, and the man looked around. As he turned toward her, she swung the skillet down on his head as hard as she could.

He moaned and held his head as he staggered toward the table. She jumped down from the chair as he groaned and lost consciousness.

Still holding the skillet, she rushed through the clock shop.

Outside, a wagon pulled by a team of horses drove by. Women dressed in old-fashioned Wild West clothes strolled along the wooden sidewalk, and across the street she heard music coming from the direction of a building with the words Saloon and Dance Hall printed across a wooden sign hanging from its porch.

A man in a pinstriped suit touched his black, wide-brimmed hat in greeting. His eyes were the color of ash and his eyebrows so light in color they blended into the color of his skin. "Good morning, miss. Are you lost? If so, may I be of help?"

She shook her head to clear her thoughts. The man reminded her of a ghost and gave her the creeps. *Don't panic.* This guy was an actor, playing a role, and was probably nice. There was a logical explanation. This had to be some sort of elaborate reenactment. Time travel only happened in books and movies.

Vanessa nodded to the man, who now offered his arm like she had stepped into one of those Wyatt Earp and Annie Oakley movies. She wasn't sure, when she thought about it, if Wyatt and Annie knew each other.

The man seemed as formal as his clothes, but it didn't reach his eyes, which supported her theory that he and the others in the town were actors.

She took his arm. "Yes, you can help me. Do you have a cell? I need to make a call." The man wrinkled his eyebrows together as though he hadn't a clue what she was talking about.

"I'm sorry, miss. What is this 'cell'?"

She swore to herself. The gentleman was sticking with his reenactment role like super glue, and it was frustrating. Everyone here was taking their roles much too seriously. Or? Was the man with the hazel eyes right when he claimed she'd dropped out of the sky into 1878? An impossible scenario to believe. Her thoughts spun as she weighed that maybe—just maybe—she had traveled back in time.

Mentally, she shook out of the possibility. Time travel happened in the movies. She only needed to dig deeper, find a crack in the actors' roles, and expose this for what it was, a very elaborate reenactment of the Wild West.

Two could play this game. She wasn't a serious history buff, but she knew enough to know that the telephone had been invented in the late 1800s, and it was a game changer. Most towns of any size had at least one telephone available.

She pasted on a friendly expression. "I apologize, I meant…a telephone." She said the word slowly and then added, "I need to contact a friend and let them know I am here."

He recaptured his pleasant expression, tucked her arm under his, and nodded. "Ah." The word rolled over his lips like wind through trees. "The closest telephone switchboard is in Cheyenne. We have a telegraph office, though."

No, that would not do, but she kept her opinion to herself as he guided her down the sidewalk, tipping his hat to two men in mud-colored cloth coats, with guns in the holsters strapped on the belts around their waists. A scar ran diagonally across the face of the taller man, and the other one wore an eyepatch. They glanced over at her, their gaze trailing over her with undisguised lust, and the one with the eyepatch licked his lips.

She shuddered and kept her voice even, with an edge that said, *back off*. "Where is the telegraph office?"

"Not far."

He squeezed the hand she had draped over his arm. She flinched and slipped her hand from his tight grasp as her uneasiness grew. For some reason, the farther she walked from the watch shop, the more unsettled and out of place she felt. She dismissed the irrational notion. She should feel out of place. She was in a freaking reenactment where the actors were so deep in character she suspected they had forgotten this was not real.

"I should introduce myself. My name is Rammon." He let the name linger in the air as though he was like one of those rock stars who only used their first names because they were so popular. When she only nodded, he pulled his wide-brimmed hat farther down.

Silence weighed down the air between them. She knew it was her turn to share her name. That was the polite thing to do. Her heart hammered against her chest, like a warning so hard it hurt. She didn't want to tell him her name. That felt crazy. Insane. What difference would it make? And yet her heart hammered again until it thundered in her ears.

"Run!"

She froze. Time slowed.

At first, she thought the warning had come from her own thoughts. When it came again, she turned. The man from the watch shop raced toward her, shouting for her to get down. Before she could react, he leapt into the air, his long black hair floating behind him like wings.

He swept her into his arms and raced for the alley as a round of gunfire rained around them. Screams attacked the air. Bullets embedded into the sides of wooden buildings and broke windows, shattering glass.

The watchmaker's shoulder dipped, as though hit with one of the bullets, and he let out a muffled groan. "Don't let go."

"I won't."

Chapter Eight

Vanessa hadn't let go of Greyeyes.

Guns fired like rounds of popping firecrackers. The air was thick with the smell of sulfur from the discharge of gunfire. Caught between fearing for her life and stunned that someone was shooting at her, she clung to the watchmaker's neck as he raced down the narrow street.

Greyeyes let out a gritted moan as his shoulder dipped for the second time. Had he been shot?

The gunfire ceased as quickly as it had begun. Silence rang in her ears as the watchmaker set her down but kept his hold on her arm as though she might bolt like a frightened animal. He was not that far off track. But where would she run? The last time she'd taken off hadn't worked out that well.

The absence of sound was deafening and almost worse than the noise. Vanessa gulped in air, realizing she'd been holding her breath. The whole experience felt surreal. They were a short distance from the sidewalk where the gunfire had erupted, although it had felt as though he carried her much farther. He kept his hand on her, but she felt the absence of his arms, holding her in their protective embrace, like a loss. She rubbed her arms to chase away the goosebumps.

She shivered. She was chilled to the bone.

"You're as cold as ice." His voice was deep,

vibrating like an echo in a canyon.

"Not the first time someone has said that about me." The words escaped before she had a chance to pull them back. She'd been called an ice queen so many times by the few men she'd dated that she'd started viewing the label as a compliment. He cocked an eyebrow, but she waved away his confused expression. "Ignore me."

"That's very hard to do." He shrugged off his coat and pulled it around her shoulders. It radiated warmth and the scent of pine and fresh air.

Pulling the coat around her, she took another steadying breath to ward off panic. She and her mother may not have lived the most stable of lives, but at least they'd never encountered gunslingers. They had other issues. They never stayed in a place long enough for Vanessa to develop friends. On a moment's notice, her mother would pack all their belongings and they'd leave, sometimes in the middle of the night, to catch a plane or train. The only explanation her mother gave was that it was time to go.

When Vanessa was younger, she thought her mother feared she was being hunted. As Vanessa grew older, she settled on the possibility that her mother may not have been well mentally, and that her fears were imaginary.

She blew on her hands as the watchmaker stood beside her like her personal guard. He seemed like he was waiting for something.

People from the town poured out of doorways onto the sidewalks. Through the crush of people, she saw someone dressed similar to the other men in town take the two gunmen into custody. A glint of silver on his vest caught the afternoon light. The shape resembled a star, which would identify the man as the town's sheriff. The gunmen were disarmed, cuffed, and led away. But the man named Rammon had vanished. Only the watchmaker remained at her side. She thought absently that she should probably know his name.

The watchmaker leaned in. "We should go. Are you able to walk?"

She bristled. He might have saved her from being shot, but she was not the damsel in distress type, nor did she want to go with him. She wanted to leave…and go where? Well, she'd figure it out. The one thing she knew for sure was that she wanted out of this western town, and fast.

Pulling to her full height of five feet four inches, she met his eyes and opened her mouth to give him a piece of her mind. Her mouth clamped shut. Near his right shoulder, blood stained his dark shirt a deep ebony black. "You've been shot."

He covered the wound with his hand and shrugged. "The bullet went clean through. I'll be fine. I heal fast."

"Let me guess. You're some sort of a superhero."

He cocked an eyebrow. "Superhero?"

"You know, someone who is around to save the day, rescue people, defeat the bad guys. A person who possesses superhuman powers that defy reality, like the ability to fly, shoot lasers out of their eyes, lift buildings. Superhero."

His expression relaxed, and his beautiful eyes lightened to soft, warm amber. "Do you have many of these…superheroes, in your world?"

She was about to tell him there were men and women who were everyday people who did extraordinary acts of bravery and kindness, but mostly—and unfortunately, in her opinion—the superhero label was reserved for imaginary comic book characters. But just then a door opened across the alley.

A middle-aged woman, wearing a royal blue calico dress burst into view. Her face was round and rosy pink, and her eyes were etched in concern. "There you dears are. What a fright those men caused! Thank the good Lord Mr. Greyeyes was there to save you." She held out her hand to the watchmaker and pumped it several times before releasing it. "We've not met formally, Mr. Greyeyes, but your reputation precedes you. I've heard great things about you and your watch shop. You have the reputation of being an excellent repairman with a fair and honest price. And of course, your wonderful mother and sister are crazy about my pies."

The watchmaker inclined his head, guiding Vanessa around the woman. "They do love your pies, Mrs. Donovan. But if you'll excuse me, we have to go."

Mrs. Donovan blocked his path. "You must call me Molly. And where are my manners? This must be the woman your mother mentioned before she and your sister left to visit friends in the north." Molly stretched out her hand to Vanessa. "My name is Molly, and Mr. Greyeyes' mother didn't tell me much about you, other than you and her son were married by proxy. Welcome to our little town. Although I apologize for the reception. What must you think of us? You must want to run right back to your home in Boston. But I assure you, first impressions are not always what they seem. Guns are not allowed in town, and our sheriff is extremely strict about that. We are proud of Wylder.

We have a train station, a boarding house that is the finest for miles around, a newspaper office…"

"Married?" Vanessa managed under her breath, shivering again, zeroing in on the word. What was happening? The longer she was here, the stranger it all became. For a split moment she'd forgotten that this Mr. Greyeyes person had kidnapped her. Focus.

Molly continued listing the town's attributes as though she were a tour guide. Vanessa tried to cling to the idea that she had somehow ended up in a reenactment festival, but the gunshots had been too real. Everything was too real. She felt like she'd dropped into a nightmare with no end in sight and it made her dizzy. "I'm…"

Her legs buckled.

****

Vanessa awoke, propped up in an overstuffed chair by a fireplace in some sort of small café. This passing out at the least provocation was getting on her last nerve. What was wrong with her? On the positive side, the café was warm and cozy, and smelled of baking bread, cinnamon, cloves, and nutmeg. All the tables were occupied with customers, and conversations hummed around the room like happy bees in a field of wildflowers.

She scooted back in the chair until she was sitting straighter and pressed her lips together. At least someone was happy. The watchmaker sat to her right, and Molly stood hovering next to him. They were waiting for her to speak. Well, they could wait a little longer.

She reviewed everything that had happened to her, like scenes in a movie. Everything after meeting the woman and her daughter at the Pike Place Market seemed like a bad dream. She'd awakened on a bed belonging to a handsome stranger. She had hit him over the head. Escaped. Met another guy, who made her skin crawl. Then she'd been caught in the crossfire of an old-fashioned gunfight. Last, but not least, she'd been saved by the handsome stranger.

If that wasn't enough, she'd fainted...again. She never fainted. What was happening to her? If this was a dream, she wanted to wake up...now! She pinched herself, but nothing happened except, of course, the jolt of pain. There had to be another plausible explanation.

"I apologize," Vanessa blurted. "I don't know why I keep fainting. I never faint."

"Praise the Lord, she's back with us." Molly loomed over her like a mother hen. "And don't worry your pretty head about fainting, dear. I've swooned a time or two before, and it gives men a chance to catch us before we fall. Now, would you like a cup of coffee, tea? Something to eat perhaps? I've made a hearty lamb stew. You're so thin and pale." Her face dissolved into frowns as she turned toward the watchmaker. Vanessa remembered Molly had called him Mr. Greyeyes. "You have to make her eat. I'll put together a meal for you to take back." Her frown deepened. "Your mother has told me on more than one occasion that your cooking is so bad you could burn boiled water."

Mr. Greyeyes rubbed his shoulder. "Guilty, and your kindness is much appreciated."

Molly's expression softened. "There, now, don't feel so bad. Few men cook in these parts. That's what keeps me in business. And your mother made me promise to watch over you and your new bride while she was away, and I told her it would be my pleasure. She filled me in on all the details of how a newspaper ad prompted the two of you to begin corresponding by letter, but you never met or exchanged photos. The two of you were married by proxy. Very romantic. You were lucky Mr. Greyeyes was around when those gunmen attacked. I hope you don't think that is a reflection on our little town?"

Vanessa mustered a ghost of a smile. She marveled at the tall tale Mr. Greyeyes' mother had woven to explain Vanessa's sudden appearance. The woman was a master storyteller. But Vanessa didn't know how she felt about the town, and the jury was still out on this Mr. Greyeyes, but it was obvious that Molly wanted to make it clear to Vanessa that Mr. Greyeyes could protect what was his, and that the town was safe. She grimaced at the "what-was-his" part of her thought. She had never *belonged* to anyone, and she wasn't about to start now.

But everything was confusing. It was like a puzzle with a missing piece.

Vanessa looked from Molly to the people in the café. Their attention was glued to Vanessa and Mr. Greyeyes, and they were whispering and nodding. The wave of whispers hit her like a winter breeze uncertain if it would bring cold winds or the promise of spring. If she had traveled back in time, like Mr. Greyeyes claimed, then Molly's assessment of the people in the café was plausible. But the Wild West had an abundance of men and a scarcity of women, and for good reason. The Wild West was not a safe place. Except...shouldn't the women be happy she was here?

She slid her gaze toward Greyeyes. The man had a

chiseled jaw, hard lines around full lips, and long lashes that fanned over eyes that changed color with his mood. The word that popped in her head was "protector."

Molly had mentioned Mr. Greyeyes' mother and that somehow Vanessa was his bride. The last thing Vanessa remembered was the strange shop in Pike Place Market and the woman who had fixed the broken glass ornament as though by magic. That must have been his mother. Vanessa remembered reading a newspaper want ad, advertising for a watchmaker's assistant. The coincidence made Vanessa's head spin.

The more Molly had talked about the attributes and advantages of Wylder, the more Vanessa suspected that Mr. Greyeyes' mother had asked Molly to make sure his bride, when she arrived, didn't take the first train back home at the first sign of danger. Vanessa swallowed a bitter laugh. If it was true, and she had traveled back in time, she doubted there was a train that could return her to the twenty-first century.

Because Molly seemed as though she would wait forever until she received Vanessa's assurance that everything was okay, Vanessa summoned a bigger smile and, realizing she hadn't offered Molly her name, introduced herself. "I'm Vanessa, and you have a…a…nice town."

Molly let out an exaggerated breath. "Indeed, we do. It's very good to meet you, Vanessa. That is truly a beautiful name. It sounds Irish. My Da was from the old country and came out here hoping to find a wife and to make his fortune. He always said he might not have made his fortune, but he did better because he fell in love." Molly sighed. "My parents had a beautiful love story from beginning to end. My Da had wonderful stories of Ireland to tell that included the Little People and the fairies." She chuckled, shaking her head. "Well, now, here I am going on and on. I just took an apple pie out of the oven to go with the lamb stew. Would you like a slice?"

Vanessa nodded her thanks and gripped her hands together in her lap to keep them from shaking. She had remained calm during the attack, but now it was over, she was shaking like the proverbial leaf. Nothing at all made sense. It was as though she'd dropped into a story where she didn't know the rules.

Molly rushed away to fetch the apple pie as Vanessa pressed down on her lower lip to keep it from trembling. She turned toward Mr. Greyeyes. "I...I owe you my life. Thank you...Mr. Greyeyes." For some reason, knowing the watchmaker had a name, even if it was a little intimidating, gave her comfort.

He leaned his elbows on the table, studying his hands. "You are welcome."

He'd saved her life. That didn't seem like the actions of a serial kidnapper. A lump had formed on his forehead where she had clobbered him with the cast-iron frying pan. "I'm sorry I hit you."

His mouth quirked up at the corners as he touched the place where a black-and-blue bruise was forming. "No, you are not."

She glanced away, feeling more at ease. He hadn't seemed upset that she'd attacked him, which seemed odd. "No, I'm not," she admitted. Her focus settled on the people in the café. The women wore long dresses and bonnets, and the men either buckskins or cloth slacks and coats. "Everyone is staring at me."

Molly bustled over with a tray and arranged the

steaming bowls of stew and slices of apple pie on the table. "Couldn't help but overhear your concern, but don't mind those busybodies. A new face in town is always a curiosity. Especially a young woman of marriageable age who shows up unannounced. The men will be jealous that Mr. Greyeyes has snagged you for his own, and the women green with envy that the reclusive Mr. Greyeyes is no longer available. He was dubbed a catch the moment his family moved into town and it was learned that he wasn't married."

Molly smiled. "You two sit there and enjoy your meal. Is it too early to ask if the two of you plan to start a family soon?"

That did it. "Mr. Greyeyes and I aren't…"

"Molly," Mr. Greyeyes said, interrupting as he covered his hand over Vanessa's. "My bride is shy, and we're newly married. You understand if we don't want to discuss such a delicate matter. The food smells delicious, thank you."

Molly beamed from the compliment. "I brewed a fresh pot of coffee and will bring that over as well. I'm also going to bring over more bread." She turned toward Vanessa. "Dear, I may be out of line, but your clothes are so big, they don't seem like they belong to you. If you don't mind my suggesting, we have a wonderful seamstress in town. Her name is Laurel Adams, and she works at Lowery's Dress Shop. I'm sure she would love to offer her assistance."

The offer was an extravagance. It was true that Molly's clothes fit her like oversized pillowcases, but she wasn't planning on staying, so what did it matter? Clothes had never been her thing. "That is kind, but that won't be necessary."

The comment drew a frown from Mr. Greyeyes. "On the contrary. Thank you, Molly, for the suggestion. Vanessa's journey here was difficult." He paused. "Her luggage was lost, and the dress she wore on the train was ruined in a rainstorm. All I was able to offer Vanessa were a hodgepodge of my mother's old clothes. We'll check in on the seamstress as soon as we've finished lunch."

Molly's smile grew. "I'll send word to Laurel to expect you. Meanwhile, you two relax and enjoy your meal."

The moment Molly disappeared into the kitchen Vanessa shrugged out of Mr. Greyeyes' reach and whispered, "I have no idea what game you are playing, but this has gone too far. Am I supposed to be some sort of Wild West mail order bride now, with you as my generous benefactor? I'll not have you dress me up like a fancy doll to parade around on your arm. I'm not that kind of person."

His expression seemed startled and defensive. "We needed a story to explain your sudden appearance. My mother had already set the idea in motion. I just filled in the blanks. In case you haven't guessed, Molly is gossip central. Whatever we tell her will be common knowledge before we step foot outside. The story has to make sense. Telling her the truth was not an option." His expression morphed into an unemotional mask. His voice turned dead calm, and his hazel eyes darkened to black. "And this is not a game."

His words broke through her barriers and shattered. Her hand trembled as she picked up her spoon but only used it to stir the stew. "I don't eat meat," she said in a small voice, more to herself than to Greyeyes. She broke off a piece of bread. "Those gunmen…they shot at the man I was with." She fought back a wave of panic as she popped the bread into her mouth. "I could have been killed in the crossfire."

He peered up from his stew, and she followed the direction of his gaze as he studied the room. Everyone in the café had lost interest in them and had resumed their private conversations. He reached over and tightened his grip on her hand. "Promise me you'll be calm." He waited until she nodded. "I have no idea who you were with, and intend to find out, but I do know for certain that the gunmen were shooting at you."

She felt as though the floor had fallen out from under her. She tried to pull away, but he held her firmly in place. "That's not possible. Why would someone want to kill me?"

"There are many things in this world that are not possible, yet still they exist."

"You're a philosopher now?"

"Among other things, yes." He released his hold and dipped his spoon into the stew. "You should try the stew. It's delicious, and Molly's right. I don't cook."

"Didn't you hear me?" Her voice came out in a sob. Tears welled in her eyes as her heart hammered in her chest. She didn't want to be here. "I don't eat animal meat, and I don't want the town to think we're married." She didn't know why she'd paired those two things together. Shouldn't she be terrified that someone had tried to kill her? Or freaking out because she'd traveled back in time and somehow was tied to a mysterious man she knew literally nothing about? The thoughts spun, making her feel off balance.

"I hear every word you say." His voice was gentle,

and his eyes had lightened in color. He put his spoon down and nodded a thank-you as Molly brought over the coffee, then excused herself to wait on another table. He reached for his cup of coffee and lowered his voice. "We have a bigger problem than worrying about whether or not the town thinks we are married. And what do you mean, you don't eat animal meat? No wonder you're so thin and frail."

She swiped the tear from her face. "What I eat or don't eat is none of your business. I do, however, understand why you said we're married. I get it." She bit down on her lower lip. "So I'm really in the nineteenth century?" She'd said it as a question but meant it as a statement.

She didn't want to address why someone was trying to kill her. "What happens next? I mean, how do I get back to my own time? Because I most certainly don't want to stay here with you."

He finished off his stew and reached for his pie. "First, tell me why you don't eat animal meat."

The man was so frustrating. Of all the things confronting them, that was what he'd focused on? She tore off another chunk of the crusty bread. "Animals are fed food that contains a lot of chemicals, so there is a growing number of people who say that these animals are not safe for humans to eat."

He nodded slowly and cut into his pie and shrugged. "Chemicals, you say? Well, that doesn't sound healthy. No wonder you don't eat meat. I know for a fact, however, that the only thing cows and sheep eat in Wylder is grass. So unless you have another reason I should know about, you should finish your meal. Molly's right. You're too thin."

Vanessa thought about telling him that in her time, being thin was the goal. Although that opinion was changing, and as far as she was concerned that was a good thing. Being healthy was the better option. As a result, it was common to see advertising commercials with people of all sizes and shapes.

Her stomach grumbled, and she gave a short laugh. Truth be told, she was starving, and the smells in the café were intoxicating. She'd been known to skip meals on more than one occasion for a variety of reasons. The day she'd visited Pike Place Market had been one of those occasions.

She picked up her spoon. "It does smell good."

He nodded. "Tastes even better. You're going to need your strength. We start training tonight."

Chapter Nine

Greyeyes waited for Vanessa to finish eating before he withdrew his wallet to pay for the meal. He remembered that she'd flinched only slightly when he had mentioned training earlier but had not pressed him for answers. His comment had hung in the air unchallenged. That she hadn't responded both troubled and intrigued him. Was she really an innocent and had no idea why his mother sent her to this time? Or did she know more than she acknowledged? The woman was a walking list of contradictions.

At first glance he'd thought she would be easy to control. Then she'd tried to escape...twice. He was both surprised and pleased. There was more strength in her than her size and innocent appearance would suggest.

Before the gunmen had opened fire on Vanessa, Greyeyes had seen her walking with a tall man as thin and hard as a flattened rock, someone Greyeyes had never seen in town before. Anger, hot with rage, had churned within him when he saw the man with Vanessa. His first reaction was that he was being irrational. But he hadn't had time to examine his emotions more closely, as in the next instant he saw two gunmen draw their weapons and aim them in Vanessa's direction. But why had the man in the tall hat offered Vanessa help? Was it as simple as a man offering aid to a pretty woman? He hoped it was that simple. Still...he couldn't shake the feeling that he recognized the man.

He shifted from his uncomfortable thoughts and focused on Vanessa. She was finishing the last of her pie. He agreed with Molly. Vanessa's name was beautiful.

Molly, a woman of her word, had placed containers of stew, bread, and pie, enough for another full meal, in a wooden box beside his feet. Before leaving the box of food, Molly had reminded him to make sure he purchased Vanessa clothes more suited to her age and figure. He thought about objecting. What concern should he have if Vanessa was well dressed? But, as though he heard his mother's voice in his head, he relented and whispered his agreement to Molly. If this charade was to continue, he needed to at least play the part of the devoted husband.

Vanessa had eaten the broth and vegetables in the stew and left the meat. There was more color in her face and a sparkle to her green eyes that drew him like a moth to flame. What was it his mother had seen in this one? Vanessa had said little during the meal, but it was just as well. He didn't want to risk they would be overheard. To say she was not what he had expected was an understatement.

His wife, Maji, had been strong and sturdy, and skilled at spear and bow. She rarely smiled, but in those days, there was little that warranted a smile. He'd lied to his mother when he'd told her that he loved Maji and that she loved him in return. They were well-suited and knew what was expected. It was enough. It had had to be.

At last Vanessa sat back in her chair, admitting she

couldn't eat so much as one more crumb. As always, he had enough money to pay for the meal as well as a generous tip. Times were not as easy as Molly would have people think. "We should go."

Vanessa's nod was hesitant, as though she wanted to stay. Her glanced darted to the window that faced the street.

He worried she would object, call Molly, and deny the story he wove around them.

He held out his hand. "The men are in jail. They cannot harm you, and I am here now."

"Ah, yes, my protector. Lucky me."

He heard the naked sarcasm and debated if he should be insulted. "There are many who welcome my protection."

She rolled her eyes, and he had to turn away to hide a smile. But she surprised him and took his arm as though it were as natural as breathing.

Outside, the afternoon sun shone at half strength as though struggling to recover from the events that had blemished the town's reputation as a civilized place. Clouds, outlined in gray, moved overhead, threatening the sun's dominion over the sky. The weather was changing.

Greyeyes didn't like change. In his world, change meant destruction and death.

He guided Vanessa toward the dressmaker's shop a short distance from the café. The sun had given up trying to heat the day, and the temperature had dropped, chilling the air with frost. People went about their day as though gunmen hadn't appeared and tried to murder an innocent. He knew from experience that those who could take the bad with the good had the best chance at not only surviving but thriving.

The double doors of the saloon and dance hall across the street opened, and music and laughter tumbled out, along with the crash of a bottle. A wagon filled with dry goods rolled past on its way to one of the ranches, ignoring the commotion in the saloon.

"Mr. Greyeyes…"

"Please. Just call me Greyeyes."

"Greyeyes." Vanessa said the name as though trying it on for size. "I really traveled back in time to the nineteenth century." Her voice was low, flat, and barely audible. Someone else might not have heard it, heard the resignation, the despair, but he did. "Will I be here forever?" The resignation was laced with panic now.

"Not forever."

She flinched at his words but kept her regard steady.

He heard Vanessa's heart flutter against her breast like a frightened bird. He wanted to promise her that she didn't need to be frightened and that everything would be okay. Dark memories surfaced from the place where he kept them hidden. He forced them back. He'd told that lie once and had vowed never to do it again.

They reached the dressmaker's shop on the corner of the street. The shop was cheerful and painted in bright colors. Large windows displayed mannequins dressed in what his mother and sister had told him were the latest in women's fashions. The mannequins wore fancy dresses, in a rainbow of colors, with matching bonnets that sprouted feathers, bows, and cloth flowers.

Greyeyes paused by the door. "Are you ready?" He wasn't sure why he'd said those exact words. All that was going to happen was that she would get new clothes.

Her smile was small, and he realized that it was the one she used when she was just being polite. It struck him that he knew that much about her in such a short time. He shrugged away the notion. What did it matter how or why she smiled?

She pressed her hand on the glass and scrutinized the mannequins. "I'm going to let you know right now that I'm not going to wear a corset. I've read all about them in romance novels. They cinch in a woman's waist so tightly it's hard to breathe, and they push up her breasts until they'll likely spill out of lowcut dresses."

Demonstrating, Vanessa put her hands under her chest and pushed up her breasts. Her breasts strained against the thin fabric of her dress, full and ripe.

Greyeyes couldn't breathe.

His traitorous mind flew back to the night he found her, nearly naked, in the street. He'd congratulated himself on averting his eyes as he placed her in his bed. He hadn't been honest with himself. He'd seen her lush body, seen the play of light from the moon as it caressed the lines of her legs, the curve of her hips…

She released her breasts and studied Greyeyes as though expecting a comment. "Well? Are we in agreement?"

He didn't trust his voice, so he did the next best thing, he nodded his head and opened the door to the dress shop. The store was crammed with women's clothing. He'd never understood why women needed so many clothes and had made the mistake of voicing that opinion when his mother had returned with items she had purchased for his sister. That night he'd received a long lecture and a cold meal.

A woman who introduced herself as Laurel Adams greeted them with a warm smile and a face full of freckles. Laurel cast a questioning glance Greyeyes' way that was hard to interpret, but until Vanessa, women's expressions had always been a mystery. Just when he thought he'd figured out their code, he'd take a misstep and figuratively put his foot in his mouth. He'd learned silence was his friend.

He made introductions, presenting Vanessa as his new bride, which wasn't a surprise to the seamstress. Molly had already sent out word to everyone in town on his marital status, and that Laurel should expect Vanessa.

"Will Mr. Greyeyes be staying?" Laurel's glance was a question. "You are welcome to stay. Many gentlemen enjoy helping their ladies choose clothes." The seamstress was saying all the right things, but Greyeyes had the distinct impression that he'd stepped into forbidden territory where men were tolerated, and that the invitation was extended out of courtesy only. He took the hint.

In addition, staying while Vanessa tried on clothes sounded like the worst suggestion he'd ever heard.

Vanessa hesitated, as emotions swept over her face like clouds over the sun. He saw the kindness in her eyes and the uncertainty. She didn't want him to stay. That was plain. Neither, however, did she want to hurt his feelings by asking him to leave. Had he interpreted her expression correctly?

"What do *you* want?" he said, pouring all of the emphasis into the word "you." In that split second he wanted to please her. "Do you want me to stay or leave?"

"Well, I'm not going to be like Julia Roberts in the movie *Pretty Woman*, if that's what you mean. You can trust me. I don't need much." She paused. "And I'll pay you back. But I admit, I hate the idea of modeling clothes for you and waiting for your approval." She shuddered and made a face like she'd bitten into a lemon. "I can pick out my own clothes."

In that moment he knew that if Vanessa wanted every item in the shop, from shoes to undergarments to dresses and bonnets, he'd hire a wagon to accommodate her choices.

He nodded toward Laurel. "I won't be staying, but I'll pay for whatever Vanessa wants."

****

With Vanessa busy trying on clothes, Greyeyes faced a dilemma. He could stand guard outside the dress shop, sending the message that he didn't trust Vanessa not to attempt an escape, or he could disappear and return in a few hours. The latter option won. It was important that she trust him, and this would give him the opportunity to find out more about the gunmen who tried to kill her. How had they known she was here, and who had sent them? Was Rammon, and the predictions of a magical storm capable of destroying all living things, closer than Greyeyes thought?

He stepped off the sidewalk onto the street and headed in the direction of the jail, where the gunmen were being held. He wasn't worried about her trying to leave without his knowledge, and it had nothing to do with her believing she had no place to run. His eyesight, naturally enhanced because he was a Thunderbird and thus related to eagles, bordered on the supernatural in his human form. He was also an expert tracker. If Vanessa remained in this time, he would find her if she tried to run.

When he reached the jail, the door was ajar, and there was a heated argument in progress. Greyeyes had a bad feeling as he entered and caught pieces of the conversation. After the men were arrested and jailed, the sheriff had stepped away for a cup of coffee. While he was away, someone had presented the deputy with a discharge document. The long and short of it was predictable—the two gunmen who'd tried to kill Vanessa were gone.

The news was too convenient for Greyeyes' liking. He'd wanted to question the men himself. He estimated they didn't have that long a head start and tracking them down would be relatively easy. Still…

He glanced out the window in the direction of the dress shop. It was quiet. The afternoon activities had resumed as though nothing had happened. People went about their errands, and children played games of hide and seek under the watchful scrutiny of their parents. But he didn't harbor any illusions. This town was not like the big cities in the East. Violence could erupt at any moment. If he left, Vanessa would be unguarded. That he couldn't allow. Men like the ones who had attacked Vanessa usually traveled in packs.

"Mr. Greyeyes," the sheriff said between gritted teeth as he broke into Greyeyes' dark, foreboding thoughts. "I gather you've gleaned enough to learn that the gunmen are no longer in jail." The sheriff swore under his breath as though to defuse his anger. "A stranger to the town, wearing a black, wide, flat-brimmed hat and a silver U.S. Marshal's badge demanded our prisoners be released into his custody. There was nothing our deputy could do. But there was something odd about them. Neither of them spoke a word, and they gave up their weapons without a complaint. I wanted to question them personally."

"Me too." The words came out like a roll of thunder.

He allowed his frustration to linger in the air, noting that it matched the sheriff's. The sheriff sounded calm and professional on the outside, but the hard flint expression in his eyes told a different story. The sheriff was as angry as Greyeyes.

Then the description of the Marshal's hat hit him like a bolt from the sky. He'd caught a glimpse of a man wearing a hat like that one the sheriff described when he'd run to pull Vanessa out of the way of the gunfire. He hadn't given it much thought...until now.

Chapter Ten

The weather had dropped in temperature again, and a mixture of rain and sleet pelted down from the sky. Normally, the weather didn't bother him. This time, though, there was an otherworldly feel about it that had him worried. Greyeyes quickened his pace and raced across the street toward the dress shop. Fool, he berated himself. If anything had happened to her…

He pushed open the door and burst into the dress shop.

It appeared deserted.

Breathing as though he'd gone on a long run, he scanned the shop. Everything seemed in order. Nothing was turned over, and all the women's clothes were displayed as he remembered. The only thing that bothered him was that the shop seemed empty. Was he too late?

He headed toward the back of the shop and drew aside an embroidered curtain that opened onto a room where one wall was wallpapered in pink silk and the other was covered floor to ceiling with mirrors. In the center of the room was a fancy sofa upholstered in deep red velvet, its wooden legs carved into swirls.

He heard women's voices and laughter.

Vanessa stepped out of a small room and spun around in front of the mirror, laughing. She wore a black corset that emphasized her small waist and mounded breasts. Under the corset she wore some sort of sheer, flesh-colored fabric that left nothing to the imagination.

He stood frozen in place.

She twirled around again and stopped, facing him. Her eyes widened, and her full lips formed the word "You!" She stood still, like one of those ancient statues of Greek and Roman goddesses. The only measure that she was a living, breathing creature was the slow rise and fall of her breasts. A door or window must have opened, because a breeze ruffled her hair. Her face deepened to a rosy pink shade that he found adorable.

"You look…"

"Mr. Greyeyes," Laurel said, coming from a back room with an armful of dresses. "Have you changed your mind about staying?"

He swept his hand over his face, clearing his thoughts. "I'll wait in the outer room."

"Are you sure?" Laurel shouted after him as he made his exit. "Your wife has just begun to try on clothes."

Wife. She was not his wife. The reasoning for a stranger appearing out of thin air had seemed plausible when his mother had proposed the idea. He hadn't thought it through. Vanessa was not his wife. She could never be his wife. That would mean…

While Laurel chattered away about dresses that she planned Vanessa to model for him, Greyeyes' gaze met Vanessa's. She hadn't moved except to pull a shawl over her bare shoulders. He had the overwhelming desire to take her in his arms and kiss her.

He shook his head. "Quite sure."

****

Vanessa waited until Mr. Greyeyes had left and the curtains that separated the dressing rooms from the main room in the store drifted back into place. She pressed her hand against her stomach. "I need to sit down. I can't breathe."

Laurel guided Vanessa to the velvet sofa and used a linen towel to fan Vanessa's face. "You poor dear. You're as pale as a ghost." She tossed the towel on the sofa. "Turn around, and I'll loosen the laces on your corset."

"Yes. Thank you. Too tight," Vanessa said between breaths of air.

What was she thinking? She'd been here less than twenty-four hours, and already she was accepting the insane notion that she'd traveled back in time and was trying to blend in. Women wore corsets in this century, and despite her first instinct to rebel, she'd gone along when the shop woman advised them as the latest fashion from Paris. They, along with an assortment of clothes, had been made for one of the ladies in town a few months ago but donated to the shop when the woman left on her honeymoon suddenly.

If Vanessa was being honest, however, it wasn't until Laurel dropped the hint that a corset made a women's body more attractive to men that Vanessa abandoned her protests about trying on one.

Her mother always said that one of Vanessa's greatest strengths was that she was adaptable. But the compliment was a double-edged sword. It meant that Vanessa didn't complain when they moved from place to place, never staying long enough to set down roots.

Adaptable.

She'd learned to loath that word. It meant

accepting whatever the fates tossed her way. But the Irish goddess of fate was Morrigan, and she was also the goddess of war and rebellion.

Vanessa pressed her hand against the corset at her waist. "Actually, I want to take this contraption off."

Laurel set to work with a nod, humming as she pulled the laces out of the eyelets. When she was done, she removed the corset and set it aside.

Vanessa took a deep, refreshing breath. "That feels so much better. Thank you."

"You are very welcome. Now, why don't you tell me what's going on with you and Mr. Greyeyes?"

Vanessa hid her shock at the question by turning away and making a show of rummaging through the dresses the shop woman had brought in for her to try on. Vanessa needed to buy time to figure out how to answer the shop woman's question. The selection of dresses ranged from high-cut conservative brown check to plunging ball gowns. She lingered over a green ball gown, then settled on the check. She'd thought she'd done a good job of faking that she belonged here. Obviously, she was mistaken and had lost some of the skill of blending in that she'd acquired over the years. She needed to up her game.

Laurel's question was curious, though. What was she really asking? Did she think it strange that Vanessa had not wanted her fake husband to help select her clothes? Or was it something else? The story Mr. Greyeyes' mother had spread was that her son had married Vanessa by proxy and that they hadn't met until she'd arrived by train last night. All Vanessa had to do was play up the fact that they were virtual strangers.

Satisfied with how she would proceed, she held up the check dress. "I'll try on this one, and regarding Mr. Greyeyes, it's true that we corresponded by letter, but there is still a lot we don't know about each other. There's really nothing going on. I am grateful that Mr. Greyeyes is a patient man, however. We're taking it slow."

Laurel lifted an eyebrow. "Patient? Interesting. He never struck me as the patient type. No matter. But by the look the two of you exchanged earlier, I'd say things aren't going all that slow. It's obvious the two of you are attracted to each other. That's plain as the nose on your face. And if any man as delicious as Mr. Greyeyes looked me over the way Mr. Greyeyes did you," Laurel said, adding a wink, "we'd be having a spirited romp under the covers in no time."

Vanessa shook her head and faced the mirror as though examining the fit of the prim and proper check dress she'd tried on. But her vision blurred. She couldn't be attracted to Mr. Greyeyes.

Her mother had made it clear. The women in their family would never find romantic love with a man—or with a woman, for that matter. True and lasting love was not possible. They were cursed.

Chapter Eleven

Greyeyes was having the same recurring nightmare.

A blood red haze covered a village of smoldering cottages and blackened fields. Bodies lay broken and dying. A starving dog, more bones than flesh, lay guarding its dead owner. Greyeyes withdrew his sword. He saw the unspoken accusation on the faces that turned toward him, and in the fields and houses turned to ash. "You are too late," they all seemed to say.

A woman walked toward him, untouched by the carnage around her. Her features were covered by a veil, and the way she moved seemed vaguely familiar somehow. The only thing he registered was that she was the only one who didn't seem to judge him for not arriving in time. "It's not your fault," she whispered.

A hand pressed on his shoulder, jolting him awake.

Vanessa filled his vision. Halfway between the dream and the world of the living, Greyeyes focused on the woman standing before him. He blinked as though to clear his vison, clear her from his mind. Was he still dreaming?

Vanessa knelt beside him. "Are you okay?"

He scrubbed his face and scanned the room. He was in Wylder, in the Lowery Dress Shop. He nodded. The nightmares were coming more often now. That couldn't be good. "Did you find clothes to your liking?"

Vanessa's expression clung to the worry he'd seen in her eyes when she'd woken him from the nightmare. "I found a dress. Do you like it?"

He ordered his mind to concentrate on what she was saying. She was wearing a new dress. It was a drab color that made Vanessa's skin appear washed out. She should wear bright colors. But not red. He hated the color. It reminded him of blood.

Before he could respond, Laurel interrupted his thoughts. "As per your instructions, I tried my best to convince your wife to buy more, but she said all she wanted was the one she's wearing. For example, I really loved the ball gown she tried on. It fit her as though it was made with her in mind, and I was disappointed that I couldn't talk her into adding it to the purchases. She did select a few lovely undergarments and a beautiful lace-and-silk chemise."

The color on Vanessa's face heightened to a blush pink as she took the packages from Laurel. "The ball gown was too fancy for me. And you said flattering things about all the dresses I tried on," Vanessa said with a smile.

Laurel laced her hands together at her waist. "I only say what is true."

Greyeyes took the packages from Vanessa and nodded toward Laurel. "Thank you for all your help."

"My pleasure. Stop by anytime, Vanessa, and we can finish our little chat."

Greyeyes shifted the packages in his injured arm and grimaced as he opened the door for Vanessa.

Her forehead wrinkled. "What's wrong? Is your shoulder still bothering you where you were shot? I can carry the packages. They aren't heavy."

"Nonsense, and I'm fine. Did you have a good time?" He remembered his mother and sister enjoyed shopping. That was another thing he didn't understand about women. They spent hours trying on clothes and sometimes went away without buying even one of the items. It seemed like a waste of time.

Vanessa kept pace with him as he headed toward his watch shop. "I had a better time than I thought I would. I usually don't like shopping." She paused. "I'll pay you back." Her lips pressed together as she frowned. After another pause her expression lightened. "I know, the ad in the newspaper talked about someone needed in your shop who could read and write. I could take the job and work until my debt is paid."

He glanced at her uplifted face. She was remarkable. She chafed at being indebted to anyone and wanted to pay her own way. "I appreciate the offer, but that won't be necessary. I'm guessing my mother didn't give you a choice to travel to my time. Making sure you have decent clothes to wear is the least I can do during your stay."

She moved in front of him. "And how long will that be?" Her face was shrouded in shadows, but the tone of her voice held the sharp edge of fear.

"I beg your pardon?" He knew what she meant. He needed the time to formulate an answer.

"How long do I have to stay?"

He shifted the packages back to his good arm. He'd been dreading this question, and she deserved an answer. He just wished he could give her one. He had more questions than answers himself. "It's…it's complicated."

****

Vanessa knew Greyeyes' answer was deliberately evasive. She was not deterred. If there was one thing she was good at, it was getting at the truth, no matter how long it took. True, she still hadn't found the hit-and-run driver who had killed her mother, but neither had Vanessa given up hope, and being stuck back in time wasn't helping.

Greyeyes offered Vanessa his arm as they left the shop in silence. The clouds had cleared, and the afternoon sun was trying to shine, but its glow was filtered through a thin layer of dust. She had refused to wear the lowcut red dress and had chosen a high-necked neutral tone, with long sleeves and a hem that skimmed the ground. Her dress was more reminiscent of what she imagined schoolteachers and preachers' wives wore in this century than the ladies in saloons and brothels. But Greyeyes' focus on her was X-rated, nonetheless. It was the same expression he'd given her when he'd burst into the dressing room a few hours ago.

She ducked her head, feeling the telltale heat of a blush. It wasn't as though men hadn't cast a lustful glance her way now and again, because they had. She'd swatted their unwanted attentions away, recognizing them for what they were—she was a trophy to them, to be won and displayed. With Greyeyes, it was different. He'd glanced past her exotic shell into the depths of her soul. But what had he seen that held him so entranced?

At the end of the street and across from the saloon, a crowd had gathered. Holding onto Greyeyes' shoulder for balance, Vanessa stood on tiptoes to get a better view. Barely visible over the heads in the crowd was a red-and-gold-painted bow-top roof, in the style of the

Romani wagons in Ireland and throughout Europe. Her excitement bubbled over, as wonderful childhood memories washed over her.

"The medicine show performers have arrived," Greyeyes said in a flat tone. "They sell tonics, snake oil, and elixirs with outrageous cure-all claims to gullible people. They are not worth our time."

Vanessa heard the disapproval in his voice. The judgment was the same in this century as it was in Europe. The Romani and Irish Travelers' culture and way of life was different from what was considered mainstream, and therefore it was disdained by those with narrow minds. She hadn't thought Greyeyes would have been one of those people. She frowned.

Before leaving Ireland, Vanessa and her mother had accompanied an Irish Travelers caravan with wagons such as this one. The familiar Romani-style wagon made her homesick for the Emerald Isle. Her mother was happy in Ireland, and Vanessa's childhood had been filled with carefree days, playing with children who didn't think it was odd that Vanessa's mother talked to fairies.

"I disagree," she said with an edge to her voice. "If these medicine-show people are anything like the performers in Ireland, they are talented entertainers. I don't want to buy their tonics. I want to watch. Come. We don't want to miss the show."

She ignored Greyeyes' scowl of protest and marched forward, knowing he'd follow. A few people turned toward her as she joined the crowd of spectators. Their gazes sped briefly toward her and then to Greyeyes, then turned away quickly. Only one woman continued to study Vanessa. Her face was hidden beneath the shadows of the hood on her indigo blue cape. The only distinguishing feature was the wavelike fall of white hair that flowed past her waist. She gave a faint nod, then melted into the crowd.

Vanessa shivered. It was as though the woman knew her. That was irrational. A more likely scenario was that the woman recognized that Vanessa didn't belong in this century. The proverbial fish out of water. But then, she didn't know where she belonged anymore.

She shook aside her apprehension and focused on the wagon and the small stage in front, lit by torches. A hush moved over the crowd as two men climbed the stairs.

The men didn't waste time but went straight to their act. The taller of the two men took center stage. He wore loose-fitting tights and performed a series of somersaults to the delight and cheers of the crowd. Vanessa clapped along with the others, remembering the acrobats and tightrope walkers in the Irish Travelers caravan fondly. She'd learned a few rudimentary somersaults and cartwheels, but her training took an abrupt halt when she and her mother left for America.

The acrobat took a deep bow and stepped aside for his comrade. The man had an eyepatch and wore a faded medieval jester's costume in golds and purples. He juggled knives that caught the amber glow of the torches to more cheers.

Standing off to the side was a man dressed in a purple-and-red-striped suit and top hat. He surveyed the crowd as though searching for someone. When the juggler finished, he took a bow, and the man in the top hat climbed the stage as fluidly as a predator. He nodded for the juggler to play a handheld drum. With a flourish and a drum roll, he pulled a tarp off a life-size black-and-white drawing of an Indian wearing buckskins and holding what appeared to be an oval-shaped bottle.

The crowd gasped, then seemed to hold its collective breath as though not knowing how to react.

Beside Vanessa, Greyeyes clenched his jaw. "They use our image and change our ancient medicines, altering portions and adding great quantities of alcohol, to sell their tonics and elixirs. And when their medicine kills or harms, the blame falls on us, not on those who poisoned them."

Now she understood Greyeyes' disapproval of the medicine-show entertainers. She had not thought of it from that perspective. "I'm sorry," she said in a voice so low only he could hear, and knowing she was rethinking what the Irish Travelers had done as well.

The man's voice boomed over the crowd like thunder. "Friends, I am Doctor Glass, and I bring to you this tonic, made in secret from herbs, roots, bark from sacred trees, and the essence of the white buffalo. Its magical properties will cure the heart and the soul." His voice, already impossibly loud, rose again. "Do I have a volunteer?"

A man dressed like a farmer raised his hand and climbed onto the stage. Dr. Glass's pitch was almost word for word the same as the ones she'd heard expressed from Irish Travelers. Except instead of saying their tonic was made from ancient Indian medicines, the Travelers claimed theirs was created from recipes stolen from fairies, goblins, and leprechauns. She'd believed it all an elaborate hoax, but what if some of it had been true?

She felt Greyeyes tense beside her. "It is not safe here."

At first Vanessa thought he meant watching the medicine show, but his expression had darkened as the setting of the sun approached. He was on edge, and something had him spooked. "You don't know that much about me, but I can assure you, I'm tougher than I look. I've had to be."

He remained focused on the far side of the wagon, where the woman Vanessa had seen earlier ran as though being chased. As she ran, the hood slipped from her cobweb-white hair as she disappeared in a puff of smoke.

Chapter Twelve

Greyeyes rested his hand on the small of Vanessa's back and guided her away from the medicine show in the direction of his watch shop, her words still echoing in his thoughts. *You don't know that much about me, but I can assure you, I'm tougher than I look. I've had to be.*

Vanessa's words squeezed his heart, and he fought the impulse to pull her into his arms and vow to keep her safe. But he wouldn't make a vow he didn't know for sure he could keep. He estimated her age in the mid-twenties, but the depth of emotion in her eyes seemed ancient and sad and spoke of a difficult life. As much as he regretted that her life may have been difficult, he also knew that surviving obstacles thrown into your path made a person stronger. She would need every ounce of that strength to survive what lay ahead.

As he reached the door to his watch shop, he ventured a glance toward the medicine show. Dr. Glass was selling his bottles of tonic as though they were warm bread fresh from the oven. People were more than willing to believe the man's claims that his tonic could cure aches and pains of the body as well as of the heart and mind. But there was something strange about the show's sudden appearance.

There was no such thing as an accident or a coincidence. His life experiences had taught him that

71

valuable lesson. The medicine show arriving right after Vanessa's arrival was too coincidental for it to be an accident.

He lifted the key to his shop from his pants pocket, knowing Vanessa deserved answers. "You asked before about why you are here, and before I answer, I have a question. Do you believe in magic?"

She grinned, and her eyes lit up, banishing the dark shadows. "My mother and I are Irish, and she believed that magic is all around us. When I was small, she said that my best friends were fairy children. I like to believe she spoke the truth. So yes, I believe in magic."

His pulse rate picked up a couple of notches. Of all the things she could have said, or examples cited, the one she had given held the most significance. Beings from the fairy realm wouldn't have allowed a human to play with their children unless that human was unique in some way.

He unlocked the door. "The Irish have a long history of respecting realms they don't understand." He held the door open for Vanessa, then followed her inside and lit the oil lamp on the counter. Clocks of all sizes and shapes ticked contentedly as though nothing unusual had happened today. The uncaring attitude of the machines struck him in a way it never had before. He preferred nature. There was a cause-and-reaction rhythm to it that made sense, even if you didn't always agree with the outcome.

****

Vanessa perched on a stool and watched Greyeyes work. He seemed absorbed in repairing a large mantel clock brought to the shop by Adelaide, the proprietress of the Wylder Social Club. She had explained that a fight had broken out in her establishment, and Abraham had escorted the men out before anyone was hurt. The only casualty was the clock.

Vanessa had learned that nothing was as it seemed in Wylder. Adelaide owned a dance hall where men went to be entertained by women. The local town gossips called the women whores and women of ill repute, and claimed that all manner of sinful things went on behind closed doors, but there was more to the story. The women had sex only with partners of their choice and often helped those in need.

The Wylder Social Club wasn't the only place where things were not what they seemed. The undertaker had taken in his cousin, a talented painter, and claimed the young man was only staying for a short time. But it was plain to anyone with sharp eyes that the cousin was a woman, and that the undertaker was in love with her.

A raven perched on the window ledge, and Vanessa scooted down from her stool to open the window a crack and place a broken clock spring near the bird.

"You shouldn't encourage him," Greyeyes said. "We'll never get rid of him." He rapped on the window. The bird snatched up the spring in his beak and soared out of sight. Greyeyes went back to his repairs as though the matter was settled.

Speaking of secrets, there was Douglas Greyeyes. A watchmaker who kept to himself, but did everyone in town really think he wasn't also harboring secrets?

It was like in the Superman movies. The character who plays Clark Kent is always tall, with broad shoulders and an athletic build. A real hunk. But for some reason the people in the movie, with the possible exception of Lois Lane, never saw the physical resemblance between Clark Kent and Superman, nor did they view the mild-mannered reporter as a hero.

"Is something on your mind?" Greyeyes reached for a small wheel-shaped clock part and fit it into the back of Adelaide's clock.

Vanessa had a lot on her mind but nothing she wanted to share. She'd learned early in life that keeping your thoughts to yourself was the wisest course of action.

"Do you mind if I go outside for some fresh air? I won't go far." She groaned. She hadn't asked for permission for anything since she was a small child. If he said no, would she go anyway?

He held her gaze as though weighing his words carefully. "It's not safe."

"Maybe that's why I want to go."

He paused again. "If you scream, I'll hear you."

She rolled her eyes. "Good to know." She grabbed a handful of broken clock parts. "Mind if I take these? Ravens like shiny things."

He shook his head.

With her fistful of clock parts, she rushed outside and headed for the place she'd seen the raven. She plowed into a woman wearing a hooded cloak and dropped the clock parts to the ground.

"Oh, I'm sorry," Vanessa said. "I wasn't watching where I was going. Are you all right?"

"The fault was mine. You dropped something," the woman said. "Let me help you." The woman knelt beside Vanessa. "These are all broken. They must have broken when they fell. I'd be happy to pay for new ones."

"They were already broken. This might sound silly, but I was planning on giving them to a raven I saw earlier. My mother said that giving ravens a gift showed them you wanted to be friends."

"You like ravens, then? Not everyone does."

****

Greyeyes knew the moment Vanessa had returned. She moved toward a grandfather clock with the fluid ease of a meandering stream. Her hair fell over her shoulders in waves, free from the restrictive bun the woman at the dress shop had insisted was the latest in fashion. Greyeyes didn't know if Vanessa's hair had rebelled on its own or if she had released it. Either way, he loved her hair this way. In the golden glow of the oil lamp, red highlights threaded through Vanessa's hair, and her skin shone like liquid bronze. He could easily imagine her running with joy through a meadow, stream, or forest. She was a creature of nature. The knowledge struck him like a thunderbolt.

She blew on her hands, and another realization struck home.

His shop was as cold as the inside of an icebox. He preferred the cold, but his mother often said that most women did not. He draped a blanket over her shoulders. "You're cold. I'll build a fire."

She pulled the blanket close around her. "I keep forgetting you can't just turn on the heat in this century with the flip of a switch. I'd offer to help, but I've never built a fire."

Arranging fresh kindling and cut wood in the potbelly stove, he lit the fire with a match, keeping his back turned toward her. "Your time must be filled with wonder if you don't need a fire to heat a home."

She pulled a chair near the potbelly stove. "The warmth feels nice." She paused. "When are you going to tell me what's going on?"

How much should he tell her? Too much and she might become hysterical. He knew nothing about her. But too little would put her in more danger. "What else did your mother say about the fairies or magic?"

"Not so much about magic in general, but she talked about the fairies as though they were real. Sometimes I'd walk in on her unannounced and would overhear her carrying on conversations with imaginary beings. As a child, I thought it was cool. When I grew older, I started thinking my mother was crazy." Vanessa turned away from the fire. "Then she died."

"How old were you when your mother died?"

"An obnoxious, outspoken fourteen-year-old who blamed her mother for everything." Her voice trailed off. "Then there was an accident, and she died in my arms."

He heard the pain and the guilt. He understood both all too well. "You are being too hard on yourself." His mother had said something similar to him. He hoped in Vanessa's case the words helped. They hadn't for him.

She straightened in her chair. "It's okay. And I really was as bad a kid as I said. Probably worse. But that was a long time ago. I'd like to change the subject, if you don't mind."

"Are you hungry?" She hadn't asked to explain why she was here, and he still wasn't sure how to begin. He reached for more wood to feed the fire and grimaced, rubbing his shoulder. It still ached from where he had been shot. Odd. It had never taken this long for an injury to heal.

She stood suddenly. "You need to take your shirt off."

"I beg your pardon?"

"I'll need soap, clean rags, and boiling water. You sit still and rest. Just point me in the right direction, I'll get the supplies."

"That won't be necessary. I'm fine."

"Your shoulder is not fine. You were shot trying to protect me from those gunmen."

"I didn't *try* to protect you. I *did* protect you. The bullet went clean through, so there's no need to worry."

"Ah, so you are also a doctor and have self-diagnosed yourself. That wound is probably infected, and in the wild and wooly Wild West, people die from infection. The word 'fine,' by the way, is a terrible word. I've always hated the word, probably because whenever my mother asked me how I was doing, I'd use that word to get her to stop asking questions. I used to think about that after she died. I wished I could take the word back so she and I could have had a long conversation." She sucked in her breath. "Any-who. You keep rubbing your shoulder, and it's started to bleed again, so it's obviously not *fine*. I'm actually pretty good at healing things. Little things, mostly, but my mother always said I had a gift. But that's what mothers say, isn't it, when they're grasping for something good to say about a troublesome child?"

"You really talk a lot."

"And I never run out of words, so I'd suggest you take off your shirt while I gather the supplies."

****

A short time later, water simmered in a cast-iron kettle on the top of the potbelly stove. Greyeyes had used matches to start the fire while Vanessa worked. She'd torn strips from her petticoat for bandages, declaring the rags he produced were lice-infected, and was in the process of sterilizing some of the strips in the boiling water. The room was warm and cozy, and there was a rosy glow that gave off the impression that he and Vanessa were the only ones left alone in town. The comfortable feeling made him uneasy. He shouldn't feel this relaxed around her. This wasn't like him. He distrusted everyone and everything. That philosophy had kept him alive. So why did he trust Vanessa?

She removed one of the strips from the water and waved it in the air to cool. "Time to take off your shirt. I need to clean the wound before it's bandaged." She winked. "I promise not to swoon."

Was she flirting with him? Impossible. They barely knew each other. He turned from her, berating himself for wishful thinking, and started tugging his shirt over his head. He winced as the shirt clung to the dried blood on his wound.

She pushed his hands away. "Let me help. You'll tear open your injury." She dabbed the wet cloth against the shirt fabric covering the wound until the shirt eased away from his shoulder. She then pulled the shirt over his arms and head. Her gaze snapped to his. "You're covered in tattoos."

The expression on her face was part shock and part awe, and he found the combination enchanting. "Does that mean you're not going to swoon? I'm disappointed."

The color of her skin took on a pink glow as she

gave him a shy smile. "I shouldn't have said I'd swoon. I'm not sure why I did. And for the record, I have seen men with shoulders as broad and as muscular as yours before."

"Is that so?"

Her blush deepened. "Okay, so that's a lie, but don't get cocky. I haven't seen that many men naked."

"Good to know."

"Stop smiling. I have to clean and bandage your wound, and I don't want to hurt you."

He put his hand over hers. "Also good to know."

****

Greyeyes sat near the stove as Vanessa finished bandaging his shoulder, talking to herself as she worked. She talked so low he couldn't understand what she said, but the hum of her words was soothing. Their easy banter and flirtation had ceased as fast as it had begun. As a result, the last half hour had put him on edge, and Vanessa telling him to relax only made it worse. She'd cleaned his wound, telling him it was horrible and was probably infected. She went on and on about how he should have stitches or see a doctor and wishing she had some herb he'd never heard of, to slather on the wound. No one had ever fussed over him the way she had, and he admitted he was enjoying it way too much.

Vanessa added another layer of bandages to his shoulder. "You don't talk much, do you? Just my luck. Most men I've encountered won't stop talking. Mostly about themselves, though. How about if I guess? Stop me when I stray too far afield. I'm guessing that the woman and young girl I met in my time are your mother and sister. For some reason, they sent me back

79

to your time. In most fantasy, science fiction, and world-coming-to-an-end stories, there is someone who is the designated person who is the key to saving the world. I'm guessing they think I'm it. Spoiler alert. I'm going to be a big disappointment. I'm a full-blown coward. Overlooking the obvious, that I'm not very big and I'm not coordinated, I have no Amazon-warrior skills, and I'm also not a fighter. I'm a runner, as in, I run from danger at the first sign of trouble. So you were about to tell me why I'm here."

She was making a case that his mother had made a mistake. And yet... He nodded slowly. "You are a runner; I'll give you that. You're fast, too. I almost didn't reach you in time." He turned toward her. "But you're not a coward. Far from it. You attacked me...twice, and I'm almost twice your size." He turned back to the fire. "I meant it that you don't have to stay here forever. There is a way for you to return."

"I hear a giant 'but' in your voice," she said, standing back to examine her handiwork. "There, you're all done. Not bad, if I do say so myself. How does it feel? I'm worried that I couldn't stop it from bleeding. That has never happened before."

He rolled his shoulder and fought back a wince. "Good. It's good."

She covered her arms over her chest. "You are a big fat liar. I need my herbs, and I should have said words over the wound, but I was afraid you'd laugh. Most people feel uncomfortable when someone chants over them. That's why I only do it with small animals, like birds, and mice."

He watched as she put away the leftover cloth she'd used for bandages. She moved with ease and grace. Why hadn't he noticed that about her before? Her hands had been gentle when she washed his wound, and she'd flinched when he had grimaced, as though it hurt her as much as it had him. The oddest thought sprang to his mind. It was something his mother had said when she was talking about one of the old healers in her tribe. She said that he claimed to feel the injuries of the people he healed. Had Vanessa really felt his pain, or just reacted to him because she didn't want to hurt him?

She'd talked about healing animals as though it were no big thing. Was her mother right? Did Vanessa have a healer's gift? Did that explain why his mother had chosen Vanessa, or was there something else he was missing?

He rolled his shoulder again. It did feel a little better, but he could also feel blood seeping through the bandages. He'd minimized his injury, but it was odd that it still hadn't healed. Vanessa started humming, and the melody drifted over him like a warm breeze. There was magic in the music of her voice that heated his blood.

His thoughts wove back to when he'd first seen Vanessa, her clothes torn in ribbons, her body soft against his as he laid her on his bed. It had taken all the strength he possessed to pull away from her that night.

"You can chant over me whenever you like." He clenched down on his jaw. "That came out wrong."

She glanced his way, and a blush colored her cheeks as her lips parted. "I'm not sure that would be a good idea. You might be sorry. It's another reason my little patients are always grateful and seem to have an overwhelming urge to leap into my arms."

"I would crush you if I leapt into your arms."

"And I'm stronger than I appear."

The wind howled down the flume of the potbelly stove, sending flames higher. Greyeyes adjusted the logs with an iron poker until the fire settled and calmed. An outsider would observe the occurrence of a breeze and the stoking of a fire as innocent. The elements were not innocent. They always had a meaning for what they did.

He inclined his head toward her as though willing her to be strong. "As I mentioned earlier, you were the target. Someone tried to kill you, which means my enemy knows you're here. I'm convinced the gunmen were working for him."

She narrowed her gaze and shot him a murderous expression. "If I wasn't such a nice person, I'd punch you in your injured shoulder right now. That has to stop."

Her anger surprised him. "What has to stop?"

She pressed her lips together in a thin line. "You talk in riddles, as though you think I can decipher the code. Let me make myself clear. I don't have a clue what's going on, and now you tell me that your enemy wants me dead. Who, exactly?"

"His name is Rammon, and I believe he was the man you were with right before the gunmen attacked," Greyeyes said evenly. "If you hadn't run from me..."

"I ran because you were this crazy person who told me I'd time traveled. Then gunmen started shooting at me."

Wind stirred the flames in the stove before turning its attention to the glass panes. They rattled against the window frame like the chattering teeth of a corpse.

Outside, a shadow, darker than night, blocked out the moon. As quickly as it had appeared, it swept past, and the night calmed.

"We should move away from the windows."

She leaned forward. "Back up. Why does Rammon want to kill me?"

"Revenge."

The windows rattled, and a streetlamp flickered outside. Vanessa tilted her head. "Didn't you say the gunmen who attacked me were in jail?"

"They escaped a few hours ago. I didn't want to worry you."

She sucked in a deep breath and pointed a shaking finger toward the window. "I think I saw the gunmen who attacked me by the window."

A face with an eyepatch flashed in the window, then disappeared, and Vanessa screamed and stood, toppling over her chair.

Greyeyes was on his feet, pushing her behind him and grabbing for his gun.

An animal's howl tore through the night, then another howl, deeper in tone joined the first. A split second later, more were added until the sound smothered the night.

"Are those wolves? They don't sound happy," Vanessa said, her voice low and shaking.

"They're not wolves. They are bobcats. They're solitary animals—normally."

Vanessa stood and moved away from the front entrance. "Why do they sound so close?"

Something scratched at the door. A rock broke through the window on the far side of the shop, shattering glass. A gunman leapt through the open window and landed on his feet.

Keeping Vanessa behind him, and his gun trained on the man, Greyeyes edged toward the back of the shop.

The man's facial features changed first as he shed his clothes. Ears grew to points and were covered with tufts of gray hair. Whiskers appeared. Teeth elongated. One eye shone with hate while the other was still covered by an eyepatch. Paws with razor-sharp claws replaced hands and feet. Then red fur, interspersed with black spots, covered what had been the man's body, and the transformation was complete. The man had shapeshifted into a bobcat.

The bobcat growled and lowered his head, keeping his one good eye locked on Greyeyes. Greyeyes knew the animal waited for its leader's order to attack. Greyeyes mourned that this bobcat had allied himself against him. Bobcats had heightened mysticism, and one of their gifts was to teach how to be alone without being lonely. But bobcats were also easily swayed to the darkness, and once turned, were forever corrupted.

Behind Greyeyes, he felt Vanessa tense. She'd witnessed a man shapeshifting into animal form. What must she be thinking?

Most would have become hysterical, and he wouldn't have blamed them. The world misunderstood and therefore rejected magic, even if they witnessed it firsthand. Magic was explained away as fantasy, and those who clung to what they saw were judged, maligned. Vanessa, by her own admission, had judged her mother unwell for claiming the ability to talk to beings Vanessa herself had seen. Peer pressure had driven Vanessa's childhood experiences underground.

Were those same thoughts running through Vanessa's thoughts now? Magic was magic, regardless of the form it took.

Was that the reason that, even witnessing the impossible, Vanessa hadn't screamed again but remained still? Her body was rigid as though poised to act on a moment's notice. It was as though she grew stronger the greater the danger.

A gunshot ripped through the front door, exploding the wood. Another gunshot shattered the front windows, sending shards of glass across the floor.

Greyeyes lunged for Vanessa, grabbing her in his arms, and as he hit the floor, covering her with his body while glass fell like rain.

Fangs bared, the bobcat howled again and sprang toward him.

Greyeyes jumped to his feet and the bobcat slammed against his chest, driving him back to the ground. Wrestling for the upper hand, Greyeyes seized the bobcat's jaws, snapping them open, then twisted and broke the animal's neck. Blood splattered over him, while another man climbed through the window.

The second man leapt to the ground and also shifted into a snarling, snapping bobcat.

Vanessa backed toward the stove, wrapped a cloth over the handle of the kettle of boiling water and tossed the scalding liquid over the gunman. The animal roared in pain and stumbled back.

"That man…he…he…" She stared at the body of the bobcat, her eyes wide and frightened. "That's not…real."

"Unfortunately, he is very real."

Greyeyes reached for Vanessa's hand, and together

they raced from the main room and didn't stop until they reached the rooms in the back.

"Fast thinking to throw boiling water," Greyeyes said, bolting the door and pulling a large cabinet across it for good measure. He needed to slow his enemy down and give himself time to think of an escape route and Vanessa time to process. He needed her calm if they were to have any chance at surviving the next few hours.

"Are you all right?" he said. "Do you trust me?"

Her eyes were wide. "I…don't…"

He understood her confusion and her horror. He'd lived and grown up with shapeshifters and magic, and there were days when even he thought it all some fantastical dream world, filled with never-ending nightmares and monsters. But there would be time to explain it later. At least, he prayed that was the case.

He took her shoulders gently. "The door will hold. For a while. My mother warded it with magic." When her eyebrows drew together in a confused expression, he gently squeezed her shoulders. "I'll explain everything as soon as we get out of here. Do you trust me?" he repeated.

Her nod shouldn't have meant as much as it did, he reasoned, as he advised her to keep low while they raced for the back rooms of the watch shop. The rooms in the back were protected with magical wards but he didn't know how long they would hold, especially against other shapeshifters.

Another gunshot rang out.

Inside his shop, tables were turned over and cabinets searched. Then came the sound of more glass breaking and men shouting and animals growling. The men's voices were indistinguishable, but he recognized the growls of coyotes and another bobcat. What had made these animals turn against their nature? Unlike the bobcat, the coyote was a fun-loving, social animal with hidden wisdom and magic, and therefore not easily fooled.

The voices and hunting calls of the animals grew closer.

Greyeyes opened a cupboard door and drew out a saddlebag and slung it over his shoulder, wondering if Vanessa was afraid of heights. Then doubts flooded his thoughts. Could he fly in his condition?

He needed to think this through. His shoulder still bothered him from the gunshot wound, and if she fought him while they were in flight, could he hold onto her? He couldn't be sure. There had to be another way. If only he'd had the presence of mind to train a horse.

Before arriving in Wylder, he'd owned many and loved their sense of adventure and freedom. When he rode them, it felt like he was flying. He had kept thinking he had more time, and now he regretted his procrastination. Even if he was able to escape the watch shop without being tracked, there wasn't time to steal a horse and escape. There was no way he and Vanessa could outrun whoever hunted them on foot. He didn't have a choice. He would have to risk transforming.

"Do you like to fly?" he said.

She raised an eyebrow. "Flying is okay, but I prefer train travel. Unfortunately, you've made it clear that this is the nineteenth century. Have airplanes been invented yet? I can't remember when the Wright brothers first flew their first plane. I think it was in the early nineteen hundreds."

She was talking nonstop again. He didn't mind. He loved how her mind worked and how she seemed to process what she was thinking out loud. He was starting to understand that talking in long streams was a way she'd devised to divert her attention from something she feared or a topic she wished to avoid.

"I won't let them hurt you," he said. He knew he meant those words. He would find a way to make sure she was safe, even if it robbed him of the last breath he took.

Her breathing came in shallow gasps as she nodded slowly. "You...you killed that bobcat with your bare hands. We don't have any weapons, and there are so many of those...shapeshifters."

It was a logical assumption. "You said it yourself. I killed one of them with my bare hands. I don't need weapons." What he left unsaid was that he knew those inside would try to separate him from Vanessa, leaving her vulnerable. She was untrained and would be an easy target.

There was a crash directly on the other side of the kitchen door. The wards were weakening. He could feel their magic draining. Whoever was in the house was getting too close. He and Vanessa had only moments left before the hunters were upon them. He'd hoped that the wards would hold and that whoever was attacking would go away, but he knew neither was the case. He'd seen Vanessa's horrified expression when she saw the gunfighter shift into his animal form.

He hated that she might think of him in that same way, but it couldn't be helped.

"There's something I need to tell you about me. I'd hoped I'd have more time to explain." He paused. "I'm not exactly human."

She cocked an eyebrow but remained uncharacteristically quiet.

More voices filled the space on the other side of the door as someone used what sounded like a battering ram.

"We're out of time." Reaching for Vanessa's hand, he slammed open the door to the back porch with his good shoulder. Spider-like wisps of cloud covered the moon, turning the night a smoky gray. The dim light worked to his advantage. He set his saddlebag down while he shed his pants and boots.

"What are you doing!" Vanessa said, averting her gaze. "Why are you taking off your clothes?"

He slung the saddlebag over his shoulder. "Put your arms around my neck and hold on tight. And try not to scream."

She clenched her hands at her side. "It's official. You are crazy. A crazy naked person. You can't just announce that you aren't human and tell me not to scream without clarifying. I'm not going anywhere until you tell me what is going on."

He reached for her hands. "There isn't time. They will be on us in minutes. You have to trust me."

She jutted out her chin, her lower lip trembling. "You ask too much. I know they will try to kill me, but maybe I think you would do worse."

He glanced over his shoulder. The battering ram had broken through a panel in the door. "What could be worse than death?"

"There are a lot of things worse than death. Would you like me to list them?" She waited, and when he gave her a frown, she continued. "Okay, so you don't want a list. But you can see my concern. You announced that you were not human. You remove your clothes... My imagination is going bonkers. What exactly does that mean?"

He threw up his hands. "It means that I'm a shapeshifter, like the gunfighter. There, satisfied?"

"You're a bobcat?"

"Thunderbird."

"A what?"

The battering ram broke through.

"We're out of time," Greyeyes said, pulling Vanessa toward him. "When I transform, hold onto me and try not to scream."

The sound of men's shouts and animals' growls had grown louder as they pounded and battered the wood door. Greyeyes no longer wondered how long the wards would hold, he knew. They had mere minutes, possibly only seconds.

"We have to leave."

She focused on him as though he were her only lifeline of survival. "I'm not going to scream." Her voice was steady and calm. "Don't drop me."

"Never. I would give my life to protect yours." He'd responded in reflex, as though deep in his soul he recognized that she was part of him. He dismissed the thought as too distracting. Time for that analysis if they survived. He concentrated on the practical. "Can you carry my saddlebags? I'll need clothes when I transform from Thunderbird back to this form."

Her expression was blank, but he noted a slight tremor in her hand as she slung the saddlebag over her shoulder. She was taking this well. He almost wished she had become hysterical. That he would understand.

Shedding the rest of his clothes and adding them all to the saddlebag, he stepped back and spread his arms, conjuring the power of the eagle tattoo that covered his torso. Power surged through his blood, heightening his eyesight far beyond the ability of any living being. He grew taller, stronger, as he transformed into a giant Thunderbird. His form resembled an eagle's, but his size and strength were unparalleled. Native Americans considered him a sky god.

Vanessa gasped, and he lowered to allow her to climb onboard his back. When she was secure, he pushed into the air, flapping his powerful wings to gain the sky. Soaring to catch the warm currents, he climbed higher.

The horde of shapeshifters broke through the back door of his shop, transformed back into humans, and raised their weapons.

One stood out from the rest, his gaunt appearance, shoulder-length white hair, and long cape identifying him as both their leader and his sworn enemy—Rammon.

Rammon raised his hand, and all weapons trained skyward. Then his arm came down like the death blade on a guillotine.

Gunshots split the air, but their bullets flew short of their mark.

Then Greyeyes saw Rammon raise his shotgun. Greyeyes flapped his wings and climbed higher.

The sound of Rammon's shotgun was like the boom of thunder. In the next instant, the shotgun shell hit its mark and embedded in Greyeyes' wing, draining his strength.

Chapter Thirteen

Fierce winds carved through the air until their edges were as sharp as the blade of a knife. Then, when they were satisfied with their strength, they spun around the back porch of the watch shop. In the center, Rammon stood with his shotgun aimed toward the retreating Thunderbird. Moments before, he'd pulled the trigger and witnessed his enemy dip his wing. The poisoned shotgun shell had hit its mark. But by the time Rammon tried for the kill shot, his enemy had flown out of range.

Still, the Thunderbird was injured and the poison working its way through his blood. Several possibilities spun in Rammon's thoughts. The Thunderbird could die from his wounds. He might drop the woman, causing her death. He could lose the ability to shift until his strength was restored. Rammon could take advantage of each scenario. But to do so, he'd have to track down the Thunderbird, and Rammon was running out of time.

Lowering his weapon, he shook his fist at the sky and renewed his vow. "I will kill you, and when I am done, I will kill your mother and sister and end your family line forever."

The woman he'd seen was a problem, though. He'd felt the magic in her the first moment they'd met. It simmered beneath the surface as though debating whether to seek the light or the dark. He'd wondered whether he should call off the gunmen and try to turn her to his cause, but they'd acted before he could call them off. A mistake in judgment he could ill afford. Her type of magic was unstable. One minute it healed, the next it destroyed. He'd been almost defeated by this type of magic before. That the Thunderbird didn't sense the woman's magic was an interesting puzzle.

He'd failed in killing her earlier. Or more to the point, his men had failed. In their bungling idiocy and ineptitude, they'd failed to shoot her dead. They'd also succeeded in getting themselves jailed. He would have left them to rot in jail if he hadn't needed them tonight. For what little good it had done. He'd told them how important it was to stop her.

Cursing, he spun on his heels and struck the nearest man with the butt of his shotgun. "You let them escape."

His face bleeding, the injured man cowered on the ground and held up a hand for mercy.

Rammon raised his weapon to strike again but hesitated. Who was this man cowering at his feet? He had a nondescript appearance, like so many he'd encountered in this country. His face was pockmarked, and his hair dark and crawling with lice. He had been one of those who had shifted from human to bobcat, that much Rammon remembered. He glanced around at the ragtag collection of men on the back porch. Including the man on the ground, only three remained from the dozen who had begun the attack. Had the others run off when the fighting began?

In his rage, he'd expected to strike out at his lieutenant, who'd been with him since the beginning and lost his eye in one of their first battles together. The man was always at his side. Always there to take a blow when they failed or share a celebratory drink when they won.

"Where's One Eye? Tell me now, or I swear I'll shoot you where you lay."

"Dead," the man sputtered. "Denver, as well. The woman killed him."

Rammon roared his anger and struck the man again, rendering him unconscious.

He pushed aside the other men and stormed through the watch shop until he reached the front room. He expected to see the room littered with bodies. Only two were visible, which meant the others had run off in fear. He would need to be more selective in the future. He needed men he could count on in a battle.

He found his lieutenant first. The one-eyed man still remined in his bobcat form, which indicated that was the form he'd been in when he died. The man's neck had been broken. Rammon knelt, closing the man's eye. He had been the closest he had to a friend, and Rammon vowed his death would be avenged.

He scanned the room, searching for Denver. The man lay in a pool of water in his human form. His mouth was open, his eyes wide and bulging as his hands grasped his throat. The man had drowned. How was that possible?

The answer came swift and clear. There was only one reason a man could drown in what amounted to a cup full of water. His suspicions had been correct. The Thunderbird might not outwardly be aware of the woman's inner power, but something within him knew he must protect her. Rammon had not counted on the Thunderbird to be so committed to her so quickly. That was worrisome as well. But for her to come into her power so fast was also a problem.

He stood and moved toward the grandfather clock that had continued to tick through all the destruction. Like the clock, he would prevail. Had the woman realized she could kill, or had it been an accident? Had she stayed long enough to realize the man was dead? All questions that needed answers. No matter. She had taken a life. He'd hoped to be the one to awaken her powers. There was still time.

"Justice will be mine," he said aloud.

Whips of black smoke billowed in through the open window, spiraled around the floor, and took form. Encased in black robes fashioned from raven's wings, a tall woman with long white hair appeared before Rammon. She had narrowed eyes, devoid of emotion. "Justice will never be yours. She, like her sister-goddess, cannot be summoned. Revenge is the master you seek."

"Merletta," Rammon said, fear lacing his words. He had not realized she was watching, judging. "Have you come to help or hinder?"

"You are fortunate today. It amuses me to help."

Chapter Fourteen

High above the winter landscape, Vanessa hung onto the Thunderbird for dear life as he flew above the cloud cover. She'd tried to wrap her arms around his neck, but it was too large, so she settled on holding onto the feathers on his back. The clouds were so thick they blocked out the terrain below. The crescent moon and stars dotted the sky like pinpricks punched into black cardboard. It was surreal, like she was in a different world. This unknown world and her situation were more frightening than when she realized she'd time-traveled. At least in that scenario she'd been on solid ground. In the sky, she was completely dependent on Greyeyes.

Her whole body shook so badly that she'd clamped down on her teeth to keep them from chattering. It wasn't the cold. She was gripping the long feathers on the Thunderbird's back and was pressed against the warmth of his body. It was that she hated being dependent on someone else.

She shivered again as they flew through the sky. She couldn't dislodge the image of Greyeyes transforming into the shape of an eagle from her mind. One minute he was human and the next he was a giant bird. *A bird!* her mind shouted. Nothing crazy about that. And, of course, she'd seen men transform into bobcats.

Greyeyes had killed one, and she'd smashed an iron pot over another. Her stomach churned. It would serve Greyeyes right if she threw up on him. All that had kept her from screaming until her lungs gave out was his eyes. When she focused on them, they were Greyeyes' and still looked human.

Compounding her growing unease was that she had no idea where he was taking her. Maybe she should have asked, for all the good it would have done her. For all intents and purposes, she had been on her own since she was fourteen. There was a time when a nice woman from social services had assigned her to a foster care family, but that hadn't stuck. Vanessa had managed to escape and elude authorities. Her mother had taught her well. Unfortunately, her mother had never mentioned shapeshifters.

When they'd first left the watch shop, which now seemed like a lifetime ago, the Thunderbird had been shot. His left wing had dipped for a split second from the impact, and miraculously she'd managed to hold on. His breathing was labored, and she sensed it took all the strength he possessed to keep them aloft. Every now and then his wing would dip or shudder, and he'd suck in a breath as though his lungs struggled to fill with air.

She cleared her head of those thoughts, focusing on the shape of the clouds and trying to visualize what images they resembled. The cold hard fact was that if the Thunderbird fell, she'd fall. She scooted higher on his back, resting her cheek against the soft, downy feel of his feathers, trying not to dwell on how impossibly weird this was. One of the clouds they passed resembled a fluffy bunny. That was soothing. Good game to pass the time. The next cloud formed wings like a bird or a plane, and so it went.

Time melted away, and still they flew.

She yawned and started to slide from the Thunderbird's back. She jolted awake and reached around and this time managed to secure her arms around his neck. She searched for another cloud formation to keep her mind occupied and saw one to her right. It was shaped like the head of a wild animal, a tiger or maybe a lion. A breeze disturbed the cloud, causing it to move as though the mouth was parting, as wisps of cloud formed fangs.

The vision of the bobcat snarling and Greyeyes yanking open his mouth and snapping the animal's neck sprang like a sudden bolt of lightning into her thoughts. She shook away the image as she held on tighter. No more games guessing what clouds looked like, and no more naps.

Greyeyes had asked her if she was afraid of heights, and she'd responded by saying that she preferred trains to planes. This experience had proven her assessment wrong. She liked flying, even taking into consideration the insanity of what was happening to her.

They flew over a rugged terrain of ice and snow. The sight was the most magnificent example of nature's majesty that she'd ever seen. It was equal parts raw beauty and rugged power.

She didn't know if the sight was what calmed her or the realization that she was closer to the earth. Probably both. The mountains were real, less other-worldly than the expanse of sky, and since the Thunderbird was flying closer to the ground, there was less distance to fall.

Moonlight peeked out from behind the clouds, and as it did, she caught a glimpse of the moon, remembering how it had shone on Greyeyes' naked body as he removed his clothes to transform. She'd commended herself for not reacting. She had joked with him earlier that she might swoon to see his bare chest. Avoiding staring at him had been easier said than done.

The Thunderbird soared lower, and a glacial wind blew through her hair as she clung onto him, now able to wrap her arms completely around his neck. The realization bloomed. Had his neck grown smaller, or had she misunderstood how to hold on?

He turned to the side to fly around the spike-like mountains that appeared suddenly through the clouds.

Vanessa slid to the side of his back as he rounded a jagged outcropping of rocks. She let out a scream and scrambled back into position. She pounded on his back. "Don't do that. I'll fall."

His massive eagle-shaped head nodded, and he leveled out.

Had he forgotten she was on his back? She needed to get on the ground. How far were they going? She pounded on his back again. Mad at him. Mad at herself. Mad at the world. Why was this happening to her? "Put me down."

The Thunderbird shook his head as though to say, "Not yet." He turned toward the glow of the moon, and for a split minute she thought she saw Greyeyes' profile, not as the Thunderbird, but as a man. The moon ducked back behind the clouds, and the image of Greyeyes shifted back to the Thunderbird's and held. She shook her head. She must have imagined she saw his human face.

The Thunderbird picked up speed as though time was running out. Shadows moved over the landscape. A herd of buffalo galloped below, and the sound of a lone wolf called to the moon. Were any of the animals she saw below like those who'd attacked them? More importantly, were the people and shapeshifters who'd broken into Greyeyes' watch shop chasing them?

Her world had been so simple before she'd traveled back in time. Humans were human and animals, animal. Or maybe she hadn't paid attention, too lost in her own fog, believing the world revolved around her wants and needs. Her mother had tried to tell her. She just hadn't listened.

The snow-capped mountains loomed before her like angry gray-and-white giants. Horizontal splits in the stone surface of the mountains resembled deep scars and age lines on a person's face. Rock ledges jutted out in defiance and cave entrances dotted the mountainside like eyes on a many-headed monster. It was not a welcoming place. She spied a clearing and prayed that was where they were headed.

As though reading her mind, the Thunderbird's wings formed a V, gliding them in the direction of the snow-covered clearing. The tops of pine and aspen trees sped past in a blur of forest green. Herds of deer raced beneath the shadow of the Thunderbird as birds veered out of Greyeyes' path. They were coming in too fast. She didn't know how she knew that, but she did.

"Slow down," she shouted. "We're going to crash."

"Hold on tight."

It registered that he'd spoken out loud. His words sounded hollow and strained and blared like a warning alarm in Vanessa's head. He couldn't slow down. He had been injured more severely than he'd admitted and was losing control. She could hear it in his voice.

In the next instant Greyeyes shifted back into his human form and they plummeted to earth.

Vanessa bit down on her lip until it bled. They were dropping like dead weight. Adrenalin pumped through her veins. The rush kept her thoughts from spinning. One minute she was clinging to the feathered back of a giant Thunderbird, and the next she was holding onto the shoulders of a man. They spun past the clearing and headed toward a mountain range.

She bit back a scream.

People say when faced with death a person's life flashes in their thoughts—their triumphs and their regrets. If she'd never accepted the job as a sales representative, she'd never have broken one of the ornaments and met the woman who had sent her back in time. She'd never have been attacked by a shapeshifter or be faced with crashing to her death.

An irrational calm took hold.

If she hadn't traveled back in time, she never would have met Greyeyes. She pressed against his back. "No regrets."

Ice-laced winds lashed against her skin as she held on tighter and braced for a crash landing. Burrowing her face against Greyeyes' back, she held on for dear life. They were coming in too fast.

Chapter Fifteen

Vanessa awoke on a mountain ledge covered in snow, high above a tree-encircled clearing. Greyeyes had cushioned her fall with his body. A shallow cave lay beyond the ledge, and what looked like an abandoned eagle's nest was tucked into a niche not far away. A solitary raven perched on the ledge, but when Vanessa made eye contact, it took off.

"We made it." Giddying relief swept over her. She slipped off Greyeyes, scooted back from the edge of the mountain, and shrugged out of the saddlebags Greyeyes had given her. It was a miracle it had remained on her back. "I have to admit I was scared out of my mind. You saved us."

Snow began to fall again, and an icy wind swirled around the outer edges of the rock ledge, with the promise of more to come. The landscape was silent, serene, and quiet. Too quiet.

Then it hit her. Greyeyes wasn't moving. Panic returned in a rush and hit her like a blow. She scrambled back toward him and gave him a gentle nudge. He didn't move.

He lay unconscious, his breathing ragged, his hair matted against his head. The most troubling was that his back and shoulders were covered in blood. He had been shot when they'd first escaped, and the bleeding had stopped, but had he broken any bones in the fall?

Would the bullet wound get infected? She needed to get him out of the elements. Should she move him?

She let out a strangled sob and clamped her hand over her mouth to smother a scream. "Don't panic," she said again. Hearing her own voice acted like a soothing balm. People often said that she and her mother sounded the same. Maybe that's why she talked so much. It was a way of feeling like her mother was still with her. And with Greyeyes unconscious, it fell to Vanessa to remain cool, calm, and collected, as the age-old saying went. If she didn't, they wouldn't survive.

She gulped in the icy air, assessing their situation. They were still alive, albeit perched on a ledge approximately five stories from the ground, but considering how far they'd plummeted, it was a miracle they'd survived in one piece. Plus, the ledge was a decent size, as ledges went. It reminded her of a balcony in one of the apartments she and her mother had stayed in for a few months. It was large enough to accommodate a kitchen-size table with four chairs, with room for two lounge chairs.

She glanced over at Greyeyes. Even in pain, he'd managed to land safely. He'd promised he'd protect her, and he'd kept his promise. The landing might not have been the most ideal, but they were each in one piece. The next step was hers.

More good news. The shallow cave was large enough to provide shelter from the approaching storm. She'd worry about food and water later. The first order of business was moving Greyeyes out of the cold and tending to his wounds.

The problem was that he was a man-mountain. Could she drag him? She scanned the length of his naked body, trying to be as clinical as she could. Not an easy task. She'd heard that, in times of crisis, people would forget that someone was gorgeous, or that they were attracted to them, and just work on survival. Her face warmed as she tried to dispassionately examine his sexy bottom and muscular thighs.

Obviously, she was not one of those people.

She squared her shoulders and refocused. They needed to get out of the elements, and since he was dead-weight, it would be like dragging a nearly seven-foot solid marble statue. She had no other choice. But first, she had to stop the bleeding.

She knelt beside him, brushing damp hair from his forehead. Even unconscious, the effort to keep them in the air was evident in his strained expression.

"Greyeyes," she whispered, keeping the rising panic from her voice. "Can you hear me? I need to move you under cover."

Silence.

The only sound was the wind as it dislodged loose rocks from the sides of the mountains or rattled branches in the trees below. She'd never felt so alone in her life.

"It's probably a good thing you're unconscious," she said, refusing to panic. "You were in a lot of pain, and unless this bullet went clean through as the one did before, I'll have to remove it." Her stomach churned at the thought of digging out the bullet, but she swallowed it down. Greyeyes was depending on her. She chewed on her lip and straightened.

Happy for something to do rather than live in her thoughts, she ignored the growing chill in her fingers and tore off a large section of her petticoat. She fought through the numbness in her hands and kept working. His life depended on her staying focused...and awake. When she had enough bandages, she pressed a folded section against the wound, then used another strip of cloth to secure that in place.

She sat back and wiped her brow. "Not the best nurse Florence Nightingale job, but it will do until I can clean your wound. I need to move you out of this wind. Just nod if you heard me."

She waited but all she heard was shallow breathing. She fought back tears, pressing her lips together, then exhaled. "Don't die on me. I'll be furious if you do, and that is not idle talk. I'm famous for holding grudges. I'll never forgive you if you die on me. You're the first man I've ever thought of romantically, as in a happily-ever-after way." She swiped away a tear. "So you'd better not die."

His eyes moved beneath the lids as though he were dreaming.

She cleared her throat. "Close enough. I'm pretending you can hear every word and don't have the strength to answer. Eagles, although known for their superior eyesight, also hear exceptionally well." She hesitated. "Or it seems like that should be true. Anyway, I must move you under cover and remove the bullet. I'm going to need your help, though. You don't need to answer, but I could really use your help."

She roped her arms under his shoulders. "Ready? Okay, on the count of three. One. Two. Three." He didn't move. Had she hoped he would? She buried the disappointment and pulled.

"Good grief. You are heavy. You are also very naked. I guess I shouldn't be thinking about just how naked you are, or that your butt is amazing. Your other parts are impressive as well. It's been a long time since I've seen a man this naked. Wow, and I'm glad you can't hear me. Okay, I'm going to pull you again. Ready?"

She bent down, took a deep breath, and pulled. This time she was able to move Greyeyes a short distance. She released her hold on him to catch her breath. "You are a lump. A gorgeous lump, with big, flexy muscles and broad hunky shoulders, but a lump, nonetheless. How much do you weigh? You are lean, not an ounce of fat, and solid as granite. Does this have anything to do with you being able to shift into a ginormous Thunderbird?" She paused as though thinking she heard him respond, but it was just the whistling of the wind through the crevices in the rock.

"Okay, I'm going to give it another go." She bent down close to his face. "If you can hear me, can you move your eyes again? Or better yet, open them? They're beautiful. Your eyes, that is. Of course, it's not just your eyes. You are the most beautiful man I've ever seen. I keep saying that, don't I? I guess that's because it's something I feel to the depth of my being. Yes, you're physically handsome, but you're beautiful to me because you kept your promise to keep me safe. Please, say something. Anything. Even if it's to tell me I talk too much."

She swiped at the tears welling in her eyes, scooped her hands under his arms again, took a deep breath, and pulled with all her strength. This time it felt as though he'd helped somehow. She gave a final tug and pulled him the rest of the way under the canopy of rock and into the shallow cave.

She whooped in joy and kissed him on the mouth. His lips were warmer than she had expected, and she had the crazy impression she'd felt a slight pressure from him as though he'd returned her kiss.

Her heart fluttered, and she eased away, staring at him. The man was unconscious. She must be imagining things. *Get a grip!* She snapped herself out of the wild fantasy he'd returned her kiss and willed herself to focus. The next few hours were critical.

"Next step is a fire to keep us warm. The hard part of taking out the bullet in your back is that I'm hoping you'll stay unconscious for the digging-out part." She grimaced. "Horrible word, 'digging.' I warn you, this will be the first time I've done anything like this, and if you need stitches, the scar won't be pretty. I tried sewing on a button once, and it was a disaster. So no judgment. Okay?"

She swore again. "Stitches. We'd need needles and thread. Fingers crossed, your wound isn't as bad as it looks."

Vanessa retrieved the saddlebags and rummaged inside. The surprising news was that he'd packed bread, a hard cheese wrapped in cloth, and a few bowls. In addition, there were a change of clothes, a knife, a flat, triangle-shaped rock, and a blanket. The man was prepared. The thing missing, that she needed the most right now, were matches. She'd seen him use them to start the fire in the potbelly stove in the watch shop, so she knew they'd been invented.

Why would the guy bring food and bowls but forget matches? Did he plan to rub two sticks together to start a fire?

She swore under her breath, then paused as she

fingered the stone and its jagged edges. Was this a flintstone, used to start fires? She gave herself points for recognizing that a flintstone was used for that purpose. She attributed the knowledge to the time she'd watched a reality show where people were stranded in the woods and had to start a fire. Those people had bragged about their survival skills but failed to start a fire. Something about the wood being too wet.

She'd never understood why people liked camping. Her idea of cooking was microwaving leftover takeout food.

"Bollocks," she said, using her mother's favorite swear word. Vanessa held out the flintstone toward Greyeyes as though he could hear her. "What exactly am I going to do with this? I'm not one of those skilled survivalists who spend months in the wilderness with only a knife and a ball of string. I panic if the electricity in my apartment goes out. Why didn't you bring matches?" She sucked in a breath. What was she doing? The man was unconscious, probably dying, and she was swearing at him. She was a terrible person. The worst.

Greyeyes moaned, mumbling incoherently, and her heart clenched. He seemed to be in so much pain. He mumbled again.

She took out the blanket and spread it over him. "I'm sorry. I shouldn't have yelled at you. Don't worry. I'm not giving up. You want me to keep looking?" Although he didn't respond, she took his reaction to her tirade as a yes and dove back into the saddlebag. Her fingers touched a small square object and she pulled out a box of matches.

"Is this what you wanted me to find? Awesome." Vanessa kissed him again because she could, and once again imagined she felt him respond. She then cradled the box of matches in the palm of her hand as though she'd discovered gold. "Fingers crossed I learned something about starting a fire and keeping warm from all those hours I spent watching that reality TV show."

Chapter Sixteen

Greyeyes awoke to the warmth of a banked fire in the center of the ledge's shallow cave. His first thought was for Vanessa, and as though conjured from his thoughts, he heard her moan in her sleep. He recognized the lyrical tone that spoke to his heart and relaxed. They had survived.

Fully awake, he opened his eyes, but Vanessa was fast asleep. That was expected. They'd had a long night.

Unexpected, however, was that she lay curled next to him under a blanket, with her bare arm draped over his chest. And she wasn't wearing any clothes. He fought his body's reaction to the realization that she was naked. Reason argued that she had done so to better assure that they would stay warm during the sub-zero-degree night temperatures. But the primal part of him wished she'd had another reason for removing her clothes.

Vanessa had built a fire from twigs and the remnants of an eagle's nest so efficiently that the banked fire still warmed the cave. There were also indications that she'd boiled snow, for water to clean his wound, in one of the containers from his saddlebags. She'd saved him. Correction—she'd saved them both.

Beyond the rock ledge, beyond the mountain ridge, the sun began its rise over the horizon in ribbons of pale pink against a crystal-blue sky. With the beauty, his memory of the events returned in a rush…

Narrowly escaping Rammon and his shapeshifters. Being shot. Then gut-wrenching panic when he realized he was losing control of his Thunderbird powers and might not be able to save Vanessa.

And yet, here she was, sleeping peacefully and heartbreakingly beautiful, untouched by the horror and the plunge from the sky.

He took a few cautious breaths to test a theory, and when the effort resulted in a twinge of pain, it confirmed he'd cracked a few ribs in the fall. He reasoned he had managed to cushion Vanessa's fall with his body. Still, she could have been injured or succumbed to fear at their predicament. Her inner strength continued to amaze him. It burned brighter than stars in a clear night sky.

She had faced unspeakable danger with courage. He let out a sigh of relief, then winced again as pain shot through his shoulder. She had bandaged the wound, and although it had stopped bleeding, and the pain lessened substantially, the injury was a reminder of how close Rammon had come to killing him. Killing them both. The only logical explanation was that Rammon had coated the shotgun shell in a magic poison.

Greyeyes chided himself for not realizing the depth that Rammon would sink to in order to achieve his goal, and Greyeyes vowed to be better prepared the next time he confronted his sworn enemy. His life and the fate of those he loved was not all that hung in the balance. He needed to protect Vanessa at any cost. The realization struck him, like a physical blow, that his ardent desire to protect her went past her possible connection to helping save his world. It was more, and that scared him more than any battle he had faced, any enemy he had fought.

There was no denying they were connected as though it had been preordained. But even if that were true, there was another more urgent reason that drove him to protect her. He knew he was falling in love with her—had been since the moment they first met.

The realization both warmed and chilled him to his very core.

He knew without a doubt he'd made it this far because of Vanessa. Her presence had made him want to keep going. There was a quiet strength about her that calmed and encouraged. He knew he was the jump-first-and-think-later sort. Her presence was a reminder that there were other ways of dealing with adversity.

She was also calm under pressure. If he had bled to death, or died in the fall, what would have become of Vanessa? How long would she have survived in this isolated terrain without him?

Seeing how she'd handled events since she arrived, he wagered there was nothing she couldn't do once she set her mind to the task. She was a remarkable woman. He had underestimated her and wondered how many people had done the same thing over the years.

He had only a vague memory of what had happened in the moments before he transformed and fell from the sky. He remembered Vanessa's voice, clear and comforting, and remnants of her conversation. Some of her words were confusing, others provocative, and some threatened to melt the glacial ice around his heart. Every word, every voiced frustration, reflected her fathomless strength and courage. She would never give up.

But was the concern for him merely born from his injury and her nurturing nature? Would she have done the same for any wounded animal, man or beast? She might not feel the same burning need that he did.

It changed nothing if she did not feel the same. In truth, it would be less complicated.

He drank in Vanessa's delicate features that, even in sleep, did not mask her kindness, her courage. If he took a chance, and leaned in to kiss her heart-shaped lips, would she wake or believe she was dreaming that someone caressed her, made love to her?

Would she accept his kiss? Or push him away?

Both held heartache. If they survived the battle to come, she would return to her world. Better if she pushed him away.

But even as a chilled breeze blew over snow-tipped peaks, the sun rose over the horizon in vibrant golds and reds, promising the warmth of a new day, a new beginning.

He drew the blanket over her shoulders, longing to kiss the perfection of her skin as he brushed a silken strand of hair from her forehead. The gentle touch had her sighing, as she snuggled against him, and the corners of her mouth lifted. The sound of her sighs and her contented expression went straight to his heart.

She stretched in his arms, and her naked body pressed against him. "You're awake." Her voice was husky with sleep as she yawned again. "How do you feel?"

Horny as hell, he wanted to shout. Instead, he cleared his throat, then cleared it again. "You are naked."

A rose-pink blush tinted her skin. She pulled the blanket higher. "I can explain. It was freezing in the cave, although right now it's warm and toasty. I wasn't sure I could keep the fire burning all night. I once heard that the best way to keep warm was skin-to-skin contact. Hope you don't mind?"

He grinned, feeling his blood begin to simmer. "Is that a trick question?"

"I guess it is." She tucked his warrior braid behind his ear, and as she did, the blanket drifted off her shoulder, exposing skin he longed to touch, to taste.

He clenched his fists in the folds of the blanket to keep them from reaching out and pulling her toward him. Did the woman realize his blood had begun to burn, to boil? He ached to tell her that he desired her more than any woman he had ever known. Could she read his thoughts? Did she want him as much as he wanted her?

He pressed forward on safer ground. "Thank you for tending my wounds."

She pressed her hand over his heart and moved closer as the blanket slipped down to rest on the curve of full breasts. "Is discussing how I tended your wounds really what you want to talk about, my brave warrior?"

He trailed his fingers over the mounds of her breasts, teased the nubs with his thumb, and watched her eyes darken with desire as his own passion and need rose. "I would talk of your courage, your beauty, your soft, silken skin."

She lifted her arms to entwine around his neck, her lips a breath from his. She traced her fingers over his forehead, tugged on his warrior braid. "And you take on the weight of the world. I would share that burden with you." Her lips curved against his mouth. "My very…very hard warrior."

Her womanhood pressed against his skin, warm and wet and waiting to be touched, caressed, loved. He growled low under his breath, dipping his hand to caress her skin, to explore that wetness.

"What has made you so bold?" he said.

She arched against his touch, wiggling closer, sighing those delicious sighs as he sought to pleasure and please.

Her eyes fluttered closed, the long lashes fanning over cream-kissed skin. "Ah, that's…that's…wonder… wonderful." She opened passion-drenched eyes. "I've never felt this free to be me. Knowing I want you. Knowing you want me."

He laughed now, full and deep. "How did you know I want you?"

She framed his face with her hands. "The expression in your eyes shouted your love. Screamed, actually."

He kissed her at the base of her throat, felt the rapid rate of her pulse. "I'm glad there was a part of me that knew what I wanted."

She cast him a wicked grin. "There were other parts."

"Am I that transparent?"

"You are male."

He laughed again, and hypnotized by her heated gaze and his soaring need to make her his, he leaned in for a kiss that promised to banish the darkness as he drew her into his arms and into his heart.

Chapter Seventeen

What had he done?

In silence, Greyeyes shrugged on his clothes, and Vanessa did the same as the pale winter sun shone in the midmorning sky. They had made love more than once, and he still felt the need for more. But he couldn't risk it. It had taken all the strength of will he possessed not to kiss her. He knew once he started, he might not be able to stop, and that might put them both in danger. While they'd made love, she had questioned why he avoided kissing her, but then the intensity of their passion had taken over, and she'd stopped asking.

To change the unsettling trajectory of his thoughts, he peered over the edge of the cliff ledge, then craned his neck toward the rock face above. The mountain they were on disappeared into the clouds, but the ledge and cave were exposed. They would be easily detected if Rammon sent out a search party.

He knew that until he healed completely, shapeshifting wasn't an option, and if he couldn't transform, they'd be stranded on this ledge. Their best option was to climb down the mountain and seek shelter below. Hopefully, his blood brother Corbin had arrived. They had much to discuss. Likely, Corbin wouldn't agree with Greyeyes' decision to bring Vanessa here to introduce her to the cave to test her magic, but it was the only way to find out the truth. He would not tell Corbin that he and Vanessa had made love. That would make things more complicated.

Vanessa moved to add more kindling to the fire and blew on the embers to bring them to life. "We have bread and cheese, if you're hungry." Her voice trembled, and he sensed it was because she debated over bringing up a sensitive topic.

"The food I brought along won't last long," he said, kneeling beside her, relieved to talk about a neutral subject. "A bigger worry is that if we are attacked, we are easy prey. I suggest we eat and then prepare to leave as soon as possible. If we stay here, we'll either starve or come under attack from Rammon. Until I've recovered, I've lost the ability to shift. Whatever Rammon used to poison the shotgun shell was powerful. Hopefully, the effect is temporary. Our only option is to climb down. Even if it was a shorter distance to the top, there's nothing there but more rock and snow."

Ducking her head, she warmed her hands over the flames. "When you were injured, I was talking a mile a minute, even for me, and I said things... How much did you overhear?"

He knew the comments she referred to and forced his expression to remain cloaked. He would not embarrass her. He decided the gentlemanly thing to do was to deny he'd overheard her flattering words regarding his appearance. When he was attacked, Rammon's poison had weakened his body, and his responses were limited. Vanessa's voice had saved him. More than that, he suspected she had helped to heal him, which was why the test in the cave was critical.

"There were a few things you said that I do

remember overhearing," he said. "I remember you were glad when you thought I was unconscious so I wouldn't feel pain when you tended my wounds. You also worried that you wouldn't be able to build a fire to keep us warm." He took her hand in his and stroked her fingers gently. "And I remember a kiss."

Her kiss had taken him by surprise and was the reason he hadn't wanted to risk another when they'd made love.

"Ah, hah! I thought you kissed me back. Wait." She sat up straighter. "Why didn't you let me know you were conscious? What exactly did you hear?"

He moved his shoulder, more to form his thoughts than to test its strength. "How much did I overhear?" he said, paraphrasing the question Vanessa had posed. "I heard a few words here and there, and incomplete sentences. Mostly I heard just the sweet music of your voice. It kept me tethered to you, preventing me from slipping from this world into the next." What he'd said was the complete truth. Without Vanessa, he would not have survived.

"I'm not sure I believe you one hundred percent," she said, as a soft blush caressed her cheeks. "I think you might be trying to protect my feelings. I said some embarrassing things. But I like that you didn't think the sound of my voice was annoying, or that I talked too much." She glanced down at the hand he held in his as a smile teased the corners of her mouth. "For the record, I kissed you twice, and I felt you return the kiss."

He froze. How had the second kiss escaped his notice?

"A third kiss might seal our fate."

She pulled back her hand. "Is that why you didn't want to kiss me when we made love? And what does 'sealing our fate' even mean?" Her eyes held a depth of trust he'd never encountered before. A level of trust he prayed she would never regret.

He was drawn to this woman in ways he didn't understand. He'd never felt this way before. Was this how a person felt when they met their soulmate? He reached for her hand again, marveling at the delicate fingers that had skillfully tended his wounds. "A third kiss, with someone like me, seals the bond between us. That is the reason I have never kissed a woman more than once. It's too dangerous."

"I'm not afraid." She took his large hand between her two smaller ones, keeping her focus on him as she spoke. "These last few days I've come to realize that the offhanded remarks my mother would make about magic were real. She was trying to tell me about a world that coexisted with the world of humans, but I didn't want to listen. I thought she was delusional, and I was embarrassed when she said fairies were real. I squandered those times with her and wish with all my heart that I could have them back." She hesitated. "This bond you speak of if we kiss a third time—what exactly does that mean?"

"It means we would be mated for life."

She pulled away from him as confusion clouded her eyes. "You're serious."

He nodded, allowing her to process. There was more, but he didn't want to frighten her. He knew she was attracted to him, and there was no question in his mind regarding his feelings toward her. He could have easily kept this from her, and she would be his until the day he died. But he would not risk it. He scrubbed his face.

"It's not just that we'd be bonded to each other, fated to love only each other. Legend also predicts the possibility that if one of us died, so would the other." He waited for her reaction, expecting… What did he expect? Hysteria? Accusations? Hatred? He should have told her sooner. They should never have made love. Guilt tore at him.

"That's kind of romantic. Is there more?"

He let out a nervous laugh. That was the last reaction he'd expected. He nodded. "You are amazing and are always taking me by surprise. This world you've been forced into is complicated, and you deserve to know all of it. My mother sent you back to my time because she believes you can help me defeat Rammon and his followers. She doesn't care if we die in the process."

Vanessa's expression was shrouded in shadows. "Harsh." Her voice was barely audible against the backdrop of the crackling fire. "And then there is the issue that someone is trying to kill us."

"Unfortunately, you're right. We should eat."

She reached into the saddlebags and removed the bread and cheese, unwrapping them. "So we're climbing down."

"You have nothing to fear. I'll make sure you don't fall."

She broke off a corner of the bread and handed it to Greyeyes. "You're not playing fair." A smile spread over her face, and it was as though the clouds parted and the sun shone bright in the sky.

"What do you mean?"

She rolled her eyes. "When you say those things to a girl like me, I can think of only one response."

"And that would be?"

"To throw caution to the wind and kiss you, hard and long. Because the one thing I've learned from you in our short time together is that you never make a promise you won't try to keep. I know guys think flowers and chocolate are aphrodisiacs, but for me it's a man who keeps a promise."

Greyeyes sliced off the cheese with his knife. "You're amazing, Vanessa O'Casey. Why hasn't some lucky man claimed you for his own by now?"

She took the cheese Greyeyes offered. "Maybe I was waiting for you."

Chapter Eighteen

Vanessa concentrated on covering the fire with dirt and rocks to smother the flames until they died out. She should be worried about climbing down a sheer cliff without the proper experience, clothes, shoes, and equipment. She had zero experience rock climbing. She should be thinking about the best way to accomplish this task so she didn't plummet to her death.

Instead, all she could think about was reliving her time with Greyeyes last night. It had felt so right. Her emotions had run the gambit. They ranged from the excitement of making love for the first time with someone you cared about to the deeper, richer emotion of realizing that what you were feeling held the possibility of a happily-ever-after. It all seemed so crazy. She'd literally just met the guy.

Maybe that was why when Greyeyes told her about the dangers of a third kiss she hadn't flinched. The truth was she wanted a lifetime with Greyeyes.

Mesmerized, she watched the play of muscle over his shoulders as he packed away their supplies in the saddlebags. The man had the body of a god. Her face warmed as though the fire they'd created last night when they made love still raged. She longed to tell him to take her in his arms again and make love to her. He'd said if they kissed a third time an unbreakable bond would be sealed between them. Well, right now she'd argue that under the circumstances she felt kissing was overrated and wasn't required to ease the ache she felt. And if they did kiss a third time, would spending their lives together be such a bad thing?

He seemed to feel her stare and turned, lifting an eyebrow. Was he reading her thoughts?

Her face burned hotter. She cleared her throat...twice. "How is your shoulder feeling? Do you need me to bandage it again?" She wanted to add "pretty please," as that would require removing his shirt, touching him...

"The wound in the shoulder is doing better. Thank you."

Satisfied that she'd covered the fire, she dusted off her hands and nodded slowly. "You probably think I fussed over you too much."

"I like it when you worry about me."

She pressed her hand to her waist to quiet the sudden feeling of giant-sized butterflies taking flight in her stomach. "Good," she managed. "I like it when you worry about me, too." She peered over the edge. "I guess we should start climbing down. You're an expert rock climber, right?"

His eyebrows stitched together as he tucked his shirt into his pants and scanned her from the tip of her toes to the top of her head.

She fidgeted with her hair, feeling naked under his stare. "What's wrong?"

"I should have brought another pair of pants for you to wear. Your dress will hinder your climb."

She crossed her arms over her waist. "And if your jeans would have fit me, I'd have killed myself."

He chuckled. "True, you are very small."

"Hey! Not that small. It's just that you are ginormous. Turn around."

He lifted an eyebrow.

"It means really, really big. Turn around," she repeated. "I'm going to remove my dress. I'm wearing pants underneath—well, I think they're called pantaloons in this time, but close enough."

"Why do I have to turn around? We've seen each other naked." He had the nerve to grin from ear to ear.

She perched her hand on her hip. "Good point. I could do a strip tease and remove my clothes real slow, but I have a feeling that would delay our climb. Are we really in a hurry to climb down the mountain?"

He groaned and turned around. "You're right. If I watched you undress, the temptation to touch you and make love to you would be too great. We'd be here for another few hours, and it's too dangerous for us out in the open."

"A few hours of lovemaking…oh, my."

He combed his hands through his hair and turned to face her. He winked. "I'm in no hurry to leave. Would we need music for the strip tease?"

Chapter Nineteen

A few hours later, Vanessa's face still warmed when she remembered Greyeyes' strip tease. Her skin tingled, and she felt flushed all over. When Greyeyes had said it was time to leave their mountain retreat, she hadn't wanted to go. Thoughts of their lovemaking tumbled in her thoughts, and it had been a miracle she'd been able to focus while climbing down the mountain. For the most part, the descent had been a blur. There was the time a few ravens had squawked in protest when she and Greyeyes passed too close to their nest, causing small rocks to tumble down the face of the cliff, but that had been the sum total of the excitement.

She'd hoped the weather would be warmer the farther down they went, but that hadn't been the case. The air had a bite to it and awakened her like a bucket of cold water. The farther away they traveled from the sanctuary where they had made love, the more the reality of her situation closed in.

Greyeyes stood directly below her on the ground, a loveable grin on his face as he held out his arms. "I'll catch you," he shouted.

She hesitated, gripping the outcropping of rock tighter. If she jumped into his arms, they'd start kissing again, confusing her even more. Things between them were happening too fast, and it scared her. "Thank you, but it's not far. I'll just jump down."

Once on solid ground, she took stock of the clearing as Greyeyes stood nearby. He was avoiding her, and his brooding expression told her he was confused by her refusing his help. Well, that made two of them. She didn't know why she wanted to pull away.

She shook away the dark thoughts and refocused. The clearing was surrounded on two sides by alder, pine trees, and vegetation dusted with snow, reminding her of a Christmas winter wonderland card. A white-tailed deer leapt under the cover of trees, chipmunks chased across overhanging branches, and birds soared toward the slow-moving clouds in the afternoon sky. A half dozen horses, their short hair the color of warm chestnuts, grazed nearby, and raised their heads in greeting.

The serene setting seemed normal, restful, idyllic. But this wasn't normal. She'd traveled back in time and fallen in love with a shapeshifter. What next? Fire-breathing dragons?

Her mother talking to fairies seemed commonplace by comparison, and Vanessa wished her mother were here to help make sense of it all.

Greyeyes had strapped the knife from the saddlebags to his belt, every inch a warrior, dressed in dark pants and shirt. She was freezing, yet he looked as though the cold weather didn't faze him. She had peeked while he dressed. It was hard not to…all that hard muscle and handsomeness begging to be gawked at. Her attraction to him only made things more confusing.

She remembered when he had last shifted. There hadn't been any strobe lights, silver and gold magic dust clouds, or claps of thunder. One minute he was a giant bird flying in the sky and the next he was...him. She wished there had been a magical warning. Instead, he had shifted from one form to the next more easily than she changed clothes.

He moved toward her, and for some reason the calm expression on his face snapped something inside her. How could he be so calm when her thoughts were flying in a thousand different directions at the same time? Maybe she wasn't taking all this magic stuff in stride the way she'd first thought. She didn't even like fantasy and action-adventure movies. They were too close to her own reality. If she did read, and she admitted it wasn't often, it was nonfiction. When he had been shot, and in danger of dying, she'd gone into healer mode and had pushed most of what she'd experienced into the background. With things back to a new normal, her mind was coming to grips with the strangeness of all she'd experienced.

Her breathing went from smooth to erratic in the span of one heartbeat. "You...you have to explain this giant-bird thing to me in a way I can understand, including the shapeshifting animals who attacked us, the people who want me dead, and why—all of it. And don't leave out the part where we're bonded for life if we kiss a third time, and finally, why your mother is involved and sent me back in time!"

He stood as still and silent as the mountain face they'd climbed down, as though realizing any sudden movement might disturb her fragile hold on sanity. "The more I explain my world, the more I'll place you in danger."

Frustration built inside her. "I'm already in danger, so that ship has sailed. I want answers. Were you born with the ability to shift? Or was it a curse, placed on you by some vengeful witch or wizard?"

"It's complicated."

"That is not an explanation, and people always say that when they don't want to tell you the truth. Spill. When you shifted, you were as big as a house…make that a skyscraper. You were more the size of a prehistoric dinosaur-type bird. That is not normal."

"I'm not normal."

His repeating the obvious was getting on her last nerve. Vanessa wanted to pick up something and throw it at him. She glanced around the clearing. Just her luck. Everything was covered in snow. She took in a deep breath and let it out slowly, concentrating on how it frosted the air.

"Should I be afraid of you?" She didn't know why she asked the question. How did she expect him to answer?

He hesitated, which did little to calm her frayed nerves. He took her hand in his. "The ability to shapeshift is hereditary. Some believe it's a curse, others a blessing. Regardless, this ability is traced back to a feud between warring tribes."

"What started the feud?"

"Two people from opposing tribes fell in love and ran away so they could be together. In the search to find them and bring them back, the lovers were killed. Each side blamed the other for their deaths."

Vanessa shook her head. "That is so sad. And how many lives have been lost because of this feud?"

"It would be easier to estimate the number of stars in the sky."

Suddenly, a large, ebony-black raven swooped

from the sky and perched over a snow-covered branch above her. Two smaller ravens joined him, one with yellow-brown eyes and a third with eyes the color of summer clouds. Their combined weight bowed the branch and disturbed the snow, sending it floating to the ground. The snowflakes caught the afternoon light and drifted to the ground like golden crystals.

The largest of the ravens cawed, capturing Vanessa's attention. She knew from its hawklike size that this was a raven, not a crow. All three peered down, unblinking, and the largest spread its wings, hopping from one clawed foot to another.

She drew closer to Greyeyes. "They don't look very friendly."

"Most ravens can't be trusted," he said with an edge to his voice. "Some of them are easily swayed to the dark side, their loyalty always in doubt. But like in the human world, everyone is not the same. There are Raven shapeshifters I would trust with my life. We must be wary, however. One of them could be a spy."

"My mother said crows and ravens are misunderstood and mistakenly associated with witches and death," Vanessa said, keeping her voice low. "According to her, they are very social and have close-knit families. I like that about them. My mother also said one of my friends as a child was a raven. The ravens could be just hanging out, doing what birds do. Maybe you could talk to them in their bird language."

The three ravens let out a *haa-haa* that sounded like they were laughing, as the largest nodded his head up and down like a bobblehead doll.

Greyeyes growled low as he bent down and shaped snow into a ball. "I don't talk 'bird.' "

"I think they're laughing at you." She shook her head at him. "What are you doing? You can't throw a snowball at them. They are highly intelligent, remember faces, have long memories, and I'm sure they don't like it when clumps of icy snow are thrown at them. Do you have something I could give them to eat? Wait. They also like presents." She pulled off one of the brass buttons on Greyeyes' shirt, and before he could react, she held out the shiny object to the largest of the three birds. When the raven eyed the button, she knew she had its attention. She set the button on top of a large rock and moved away.

The largest raven tilted its head to the side. Vanessa imagined it glanced in Greyeyes' direction as though seeking approval, then lifted off the branch and settled on the rock. It glanced directly toward Vanessa, bobbed its head, captured the button in its beak, and flew back to its companions. Seconds later all three of the birds pushed into the air and flew toward the mountains.

Feeling hopeful she'd made a friend, she turned toward Greyeyes. He had a strange, puzzled expression on his face. She'd seen him frustrated, with a generous dose of annoyance thrown in for good measure, when she'd first appeared. She'd seen him bland as bread pudding when they were eating at Molly's café. He'd been fueled by anger and the need to protect her when he'd saved her from the gunmen and from the shapeshifters who had broken into the watch shop.

She'd seen kindness in his eyes as well, and desire when they'd made love.

Vanessa blew on her hands, more as something to do than because they were cold. This expression was new and impossible to categorize.

"There is shelter nearby," he said, as though nothing out of the ordinary had happened. He nodded toward the base of a sheer rock wall. "We need to get out of the clearing." Without waiting for her answer, he took off.

She rushed after him. His long legs outdistanced her with each step he took until she had to jog to keep up with him. This man shifted his emotions as easily as he changed from human to Thunderbird form.

"The ravens weren't spying on us, they were curious," she said, out of breath. "Or maybe this is their home, and we are the intruders. Maybe they thought we were the spies." She grinned at the absurdity of what she'd said. She knew ravens were smart, but the concept she'd mentioned seemed a stretch. She was attributing the ravens with human emotions. "In any case, they left. No need to worry."

Keeping his brisk pace, he glanced over his shoulder in the direction the ravens had flown. "I'm not worried."

She huffed out a breath that frosted the air and jumped over a raised root in the path. "Have you always been this way?"

His eyebrows knitted together in a frown as he turned toward her. "Like what?"

A list of words scrolled through her thoughts. Arrogant. Bossy. Gorgeous. Loveable. Trustworthy. She ground her teeth together. Where did those thoughts come from? This was what happened when you stopped dating. You started ogling the first shape-shifting hunk you met, then fancied yourself in love.

"Grrr," she said under her breath, not happy with

her train of thought. The man had become important to her in a short span of time. How had that happened?

Her mother believed in the love-at-first-sight nonsense, but Vanessa was a realist. What she was feeling was lust, pure and simple, and what she felt would disappear once she returned home. But the thought of leaving caused an unexpected pain she couldn't identify. Was it loss, regret…?

Fighting against that pain, she lashed out. "You're very negative," she blurted to Greyeyes to change the direction of her thoughts. "The ravens were three smallish birds, and you're…" She waved her arm at him. "You're a giant, scary eagle." She mentally sighed in relief that she hadn't added the word sexy.

He stopped dead in his tracks. "You think I'm scary? Thunderbirds protect those with pure hearts. You don't need to fear me."

She plowed into his back, and it felt as though she'd hit a giant granite wall. "Oof!" She rubbed the place on her chest where she'd collided into him and glared. She ground out her words. "I'm beginning to see the difference. You are also a jerk. Word of advice. Nice people give a warning when they stop suddenly."

His mouth lifted at the corners for a split second that looked suspiciously like he'd started to smile but thought better of it and changed his mind. "I apologize. Are you hurt?"

"I'm fine," she said through gritted teeth. "Don't do it again."

"Noted. We've arrived at the cave."

"That wasn't much of an apology," she said under her breath. She walked toward the cave he'd indicated. It was partially covered by overhanging branches hiding an opening that could accommodate a compact car. She pulled the branches aside.

Carved deep into the cave's stone walls were symbols. One was a circle, and within the circle were etched two arrows aimed at each other. There was also an arrowhead design, and farther along the wall was a grouping of triangular shapes drawn to resemble the wings of butterflies. Embedded within the triangle were small round stones in reds, blues, greens, and yellows.

She rubbed the black-and-white butterfly tattoo on her wrist. She'd always planned to have a tattoo artist add colors to her butterfly but had never gotten around to it. On the opposite side of the cave entrance was a stylized carving of an eagle. "Do you know the meaning of these symbols?"

"Many are protection symbols and will keep you safe."

He'd said many, not all. He believed—really believed—that the carved symbols held magic. Her heart slowed a beat. Her mother had also believed that Irish and Gypsy Traveler symbols would keep them safe when they arrived in America. They hadn't.

"Wait for me here," he said. "I'll find us food and be right back."

She snapped her head back toward him, panic bubbling to the service. Because of how the past few days had gone so far, the chance of there being predators inside the cave was high. He might believe the symbols would keep her from danger. She didn't share the same opinion. There was something familiar about some of them that had her concerned. They were part of a memory, or perhaps a dream, and they seemed to call to her.

She swallowed her apprehension. Her mother had raised her to be a survivor, and she'd managed on her own by trusting her instincts, which gave her an idea. She held out her hand toward Greyeyes. "I need your knife. There could be bears or wolves inside the cave, and I want to be able to protect myself when you leave." She left out her biggest fear—that if there were animals in the cave, they were shapeshifters.

"I can assure you that nothing dwells inside the cave. The symbols keep away all that could cause you harm."

"If you do not give me the knife, I'm going with you whether you like it or not."

"It is too cold for you, and a storm is coming."

"Then give me the knife, because if you leave with it, I will follow."

He pulled the knife from its scabbard. "You are the most stubborn woman I've ever met. Do you know how to use a knife?"

Vanessa hesitated, observing the knife Greyeyes had unsheathed. It was a warrior's weapon, with the hilt covered in weathered leather and symbols etched down the length of the blade. She'd survived because people underestimated her. They thought she was too small and delicate to be a threat. Her mother had trained her to fight as soon as she could walk.

"Yes," she answered, hoping he wouldn't ask any more questions. "I can use a knife."

Chapter Twenty

Greyeyes glanced over his shoulder and sighed in relief. Vanessa had slipped inside the cave. He knew she didn't believe the symbols would protect her from predators. The fact that she didn't believe him when he said so should have made him furious. He hated when his word was questioned, and Vanessa did it as easily as breathing. In her case, however, he respected that she challenged him.

Making love with her had been a mistake.

He'd allowed his attraction to her to cloud all reason. Landing on the mountain ledge had been an accident, but his destination had always been this location. His mother had sent Vanessa to him because she must have sensed Vanessa had hidden powers that could help them in their battle. But what if his mother was wrong? The test in the cave would prove one way or another, and because of his growing attraction, he hoped his mother was wrong.

Storm clouds moved across the sky, smothering the sun and casting shadows over the mountains. Animals sought safety, and in the distance a wolf let out a howl of warning. Branches shivered in distress as Greyeyes spread the palm of his hand on the bark of the tree and whispered an ancient reassuring prayer. He knew the forest braced for war...or was it something else? Did they sense the awakening of a new power?

Greyeyes headed toward the prearranged meeting place, reliving the events of the last twenty-four hours. His friend should have arrived by now. He was no closer to an answer than he was when Vanessa had first appeared. She was a contradiction. At first glance, she appeared ordinary. A woman of average height and appearance. Someone to dismiss easily as of no importance. If you noticed her eyes or warm smile, you might give her a second glance. A third glance hinted at hidden power and secrets.

She'd accepted his knife and handled it as though she were a seasoned warrior.

In that moment, he'd felt both pride and fear. Warriors seldom lived long.

There was something about her, as though her soul reached out to his, and each passing moment with her became more difficult. It wasn't just that he wanted to protect her and keep her from harm—he wanted her in his arms and in his bed.

A large raven soared overhead, circled, dipped its wing, and landed on the ground in front of Greyeyes. It was the same raven as before, only this time he was alone. The raven gave a slight nod of its head in greeting. Within the time it takes to draw a breath, the raven shifted into the form of a man a head shorter than Greyeyes.

"Corbin," Greyeyes said. "Thank you for initiating the test with Vanessa earlier."

Corbin grinned. "I should be angry with you. Would you really have thrown snowballs at me if the woman had not intervened? Was that really the best way to test her?"

"Her name is Vanessa, and she surprised me. Not

many would have reacted the way she did to protect a bird. I was prepared for her to fail."

Corbin eyed Greyeyes. "What else is this woman to you?"

Greyeyes leaned against the trunk of a tree. "I don't know, and that's what bothers me. I left her in the cave to face another test."

Corbin lifted a dark brow. "Alone?"

"This is something Vanessa has to do on her own. There is more to her than meets the eyes. When I fell, I was badly damaged and am still not fully recovered enough to shift. But I believe I would have died from the poison if not for Vanessa. She did more than bandage my wounds. Whether knowingly or unknowingly, she purged the poison from my wounds."

Corbin let out his breath and glanced in the direction of the cave's entrance. "It could be a trick to lull you into trusting her. Do you think it wise to leave Vanessa alone in the cave? Her powers could be released."

"Not wise, but necessary. My mother selected this woman for a reason."

Corbin pulled his long hair back from his forehead with both hands. "I say this with a heavy heart. Is it possible your mother seeks revenge against you? She knows you hate this war, and before the attack that killed your wife, you were trying to bring people together for peace talks. Could she have selected this woman not to help you but to eliminate you, as well as to avenge the death of her husband and your father? There are still those who blame you for not arriving in time."

Greyeyes felt the weight of Corbin's words. There

were things about his mother's past he didn't know and wouldn't ask. People had a right to their secrets. "None blames me more than I blame myself. I will not deny or condemn her for the right to seek revenge."

Corbin cuffed Greyeyes on his good shoulder and stepped in front of him to gain his full attention. "We are spirit brothers, which means that your enemies are my enemies, your friends my friends. Never doubt my loyalty. If your mother has betrayed you, she is now my enemy."

Greyeyes put both hands on Corbin's shoulders. "Your loyalty is never in doubt, brother. Thank you. Let us pray my mother had a reason for sending Vanessa to us."

Chapter Twenty-One

Vanessa removed a torch from the cave's wall sconce and headed in the direction of the musical humming sound of running water. It called to her as water always had, even as a small child. She lifted the torch higher and ventured deeper into the cave. The sound of running water grew louder, easing the tension, fears, and doubt, and welcoming her with open arms. Near water there was clarity and answers.

Markings farther inside the cave reflected the ones Vanessa had seen in the entrance, as well as on the walls of the watch shop. There were curious images carved into the stone and blacked with ash. Some were stylized carvings of wolves, bears, eagles, whales, ravens, and even the triangle symbol representing butterflies. Every few yards, a carving was less distinct, as though eroded by the passage of time. Other images were wavy, intersecting lines that folded into one another or formed in circles, reminding her of the Irish Celtic symbols carved into standing stones.

A wave of homesickness for her mother and Ireland swept over her. Her mother had lectured her about the weakness of becoming too attached to a place, even the Emerald Isle of their homeland.

She heard the low purr of water as it flowed over ancient rocks deep in the belly of the cave. It beckoned her, pulling her forward. Curious, she followed the sound of running water as it rolled and grumbled impatiently, as though seeking escape. With each step closer to the source, the cave paintings increased. Some were repeats of the ones near the cave's entrance, but there were new drawings as well. The most prominent and most repeated were the Thunderbird and the star constellations.

Vanessa rounded a bend in the underground path to a massive room that had been carved out of the mountain. A waterfall roared down the sides of the rock walls and emptied into the dark pool. She caught the glint of metal shimmering below the surface of the water, and bent to retrieve the object.

It was a pendant of a butterfly with emerald-green wings, suspended on a silver chain. It looked like... It was... Her mother's pendant.

The memory of the car racing toward her mother at breakneck speed rushed back. She was there again, hearing her mother's screams as she pushed Vanessa out of the way, telling her to run and not look back. Vanessa had run, and the impulse to flee haunted her to this day. She should have stopped. It had only taken what seemed like seconds for Vanessa to reconsider and run back to help her mother, but it was too late. Her mother lay dead in a pool of blood as the black sedan that had hit her mother sped away.

The walls of the cave closed in. Why was the pendant here? Was Greyeyes connected somehow? Of course he was. Nothing was a coincidence. That was one of the lessons her mother had taught her. Her mother believed there was a reason for everything, even death. Vanessa had struggled to come to terms with her mother's death and the overwhelming thought that her mother knew she had been murdered. Worse, that Vanessa had run away at the first sign of danger. She'd failed her mother.

The sound of water filled her senses, roaring in her veins and thundering through her body. She moved toward the butterfly drawn on the cave wall and paused. It was like the one her mother had given her. The resemblance was so similar her breath caught and held. The water flowing over the rocks seemed to growl and vibrate through the cave as though waiting.

She reached up and traced her fingers over the lines of the butterfly. Her mother had told her it meant rebirth, transformation, change, and hope.

The stone warmed, then glowed amber. The image changed as the lines grew and filled out to form a two-dimensional creature. Her pulse quickened as she tried to pull her hand from the stone image. All the cave paintings illuminated as though a light switch had been turned on, casting the cave in an unnatural glow.

Then the heat increased, and a jolt of light exploded, blinding Vanessa and throwing her against the cave wall.

Chapter Twenty-Two

A flash of light, so bright it turned night into day, exploded from the mouth of the cave. Heat from the blast melted snow from the trees and sent the birds soaring into the sky and forest animals fleeing for cover. Silence descended like a cloak of dark foreboding.

Greyeyes threw his arms in front of his face to shield his eyes. His immediate thought was for Vanessa. Turning from the blaze, he helped Corbin to his feet. "I must go to her."

Corbin kept his gaze averted from the light and nodded. "I know. You must be careful. The blast can mean only one thing. The power of her spirit animal has been awakened, and there is a dark side."

Greyeyes stood stone still, fighting against the truth in his spirit brother's words. For all the positive symbolism of the butterfly, it could also symbolize the dead or that death was on the march. The legends of his people, and their spirit animals, were rich with meaning and prediction, and left many avenues open to interpretation. This was especially true if a spirit animal showed up in a dream or appeared suddenly in your path. The appearance of a buffalo could mean abundance in a physical sense, or it could be a more spiritual message indicating that you were on the right path.

His parents had taught him that a wise person never prejudged. "Perhaps, but the butterfly wasn't the only totem represented in the cave."

The light from the cave dimmed, plunging the forest into a shade of slate gray, but the silence remained.

Corbin turned toward the sky and the smoke-like cloud cover. "I pray you are right, brother. My sisters and brothers of the sky have fled. They fear the coming storm. I must go to them before their fear consumes them. They will be needed in the coming fight." Corbin turned back, the expression of concern clear in his eyes. "But I will stay if you would like me to accompany you into the cave."

Greyeyes clapped Corbin on the shoulder. "You are a good friend. But this is something I must do on my own." He left unspoken what would happen if he didn't return from his encounter with Vanessa. They both knew the consequences.

He waited until Corbin had transformed into his raven form and was safely in the air before turning toward the mouth of the cave. What would he find? Plunging into the cave like a person might fly toward the eye of a storm, Greyeyes braced for whatever might lie ahead.

An advantage of his Thunderbird nature was that his vision was even better in the dark than in the light. He followed the path of Vanessa's footsteps and soon knew the direction she'd taken. She was headed toward the underground stream and waterfall.

On the one hand, he hoped the markings on the walls of the cave had awakened her totem. It might help her adjust to this world in the fight to come. He knew she struggled with all she had experienced. How could she not? He was asking her to dwell in two opposing worlds. The world of humans with its limits on time and space, and his world where boundaries didn't exist.

But there was a part of him that hoped her spirt animal would not appear. If that were the case, his enemies might not consider her a threat, and she would be safe.

He paused beside the wall covered with the totem images of the bird kingdom. Some of the totem images had been burned or chiseled out of the stone. Why hadn't he noticed that before? He examined the wall closer. The destruction was new.

A new fear gripped him. All this time he'd been worried about Rammon. But this was not Rammon's work. He did not possess the skill to remove these totems. They were protected and sacred and had been here since the dawn of time. Who had Rammon allied with?

He quickened his pace until he reached the large room that had been carved out by his ancestors in the time before time when his people outnumbered humans. This room was used for ceremonies that celebrated births, marriages, and deaths, and it was also used in time of war. Water flowed down the rock wall in a solid sheet as he searched the chamber.

Then he saw her.

Vanessa lay curled on her side, unmoving.

Panic stopped his heart. He rushed toward her and knelt. "Vanessa." He kept his voice low so as not to frighten her as he rolled her toward him. "Please come back to me."

The butterfly tattoo on her wrist was glowing, a

clear indication that this was the symbol of her spirit totem. But it was early in the process, and the color of the butterfly was not clear. The color was important and could mean the difference between a positive sign or an evil one—and a black butterfly symbolized death.

Her eyes fluttered open as though his words were magic and had awakened her. When she turned toward him, her face was streaked with tears, her expression contorted with anger. She held her hand toward him. A silver pendant, the twin of the one she wore around her neck, dangled from her fingers. "This belonged to my mother. Did you kill her?"

Chapter Twenty-Three

The sun dipped low over the horizon, casting shadows over the town of Wylder. Vanessa pulled on the reins of her chestnut-colored mare as she reached the crest of the hill. In the distance, the town looked abandoned. No doubt a trick of light and her lack of sleep. She shook away the dark foreboding. Soon she would be back in her own time, and everything would return to the way it was before she'd met Greyeyes. But she couldn't shake the feeling that her mother was involved in all that had happened to her.

She'd reached the outskirts of Wylder exactly as Greyeyes had promised. He had provided her with one of the horses she'd seen grazing near the cave, adding that the animal would see her safely back to town. She knew her mare's keen sense of direction wasn't the only reason for her reaching her destination safely. Greyeyes followed closely behind. She didn't know how she knew. She just did.

The explosion of light in the cave, which had emanated from the totems, had done more than illuminate the dark shadows—it had banished her fear. She rubbed her wrist over the tattoo of twin matching black wavy lines and knew they represented water. She saw the connection between her heritage and that of Greyeyes. Both beginnings were rooted in the earth and tethered to the sky. She knew she was a healer and that her power came from water. The extent of her power was still unknown. But her emotions had been raw.

She didn't know why her mother's pendant was in the cave, and when Greyeyes knelt over her, she'd said the first thing on her mind—"Did you kill my mother?"

Their last time together in the cave had been brief. How could it not? She'd accused him of murder. He'd never answered her question. It was as though he'd wanted her to draw her own conclusions. The man was so frustrating.

But would she have believed him if he'd said he *hadn't* been the hit-and-run driver who'd killed her mother?

The answer was a simple yes or no. At least that was what she'd first thought. But accusing him of the heinous crime held an underlying truth. It meant she thought him capable of the crime.

She wished she could have snatched back the words she'd spoken in the cave.

The hurt in his eyes when she'd accused him was an ache in her heart that wouldn't subside.

She urged her horse forward as the sun disappeared and the shadows grew and spread over the town as though they meant to swallow it whole. Her horse tossed its head and whinnied in panic, sharing her unease. She whispered comforting words to the horse and pressed on toward the center of town.

But it was too quiet. The town was as white as a ghost's shroud, as though the Grim Reaper had paid a visit. The town of Wylder was frozen in time. Nothing moved. Nothing drew breath. Every building had been painted the color of frost and every living thing drawn with the same deadly brush. If this had been a painting, there would have been a serene beauty and poetry to the scene. But this was not a painting.

As silent as the town, Greyeyes, astride his black horse, moved beside her.

A train stood motionless in the train depot on Old Cheyenne Road, and on the other side of the tracks the Wylder County Social Club looked more like a deserted haunted house than a vibrant establishment.

"The town is under a spell," Greyeyes said. "We must be watchful."

He headed his horse toward the middle of Wylder. Nearby, a wagon, drawn by two horses, stood as still as stone as though they had been sculpted from a giant block of ice. People were frozen in place along sidewalks, or in mid stride, their expressions locked forever in shock as though they'd known what was about to happen to them.

Her immediate concern sped to Molly and Laurel, who had been so kind to her. Her horse seemed to sense her worry and surged forward. Vanessa tangled her fingers in the horse's mane and clung on for dear life. She gulped in a breath of air and tried not to panic. She was not a rider. Far from it. The closest she'd been to riding a horse was on a merry-go-round when she was five.

Wylder was eerily silent.

The sky darkened. Sword-gray clouds moved overhead, covering the emerging moon and stars. The wind gained in strength, and snow began to fall. A storm was coming. Vanessa could feel its power building.

Her horse cantered to a stop beside the café. When she'd first arrived, the café was a cheerful place that begged you to enter. Open windows had released warm smells of baking bread and roasting meats and thick vegetable stews. Now it was abandoned. The door gaped open, and the windowpanes were covered in a thin layer of frost.

Greyeyes helped her down from the horse. But she avoided his gaze, still unsure how to speak to him after her accusation. "Molly..." Vanessa said. "Do you think she escaped?"

He shook his head. "No one living in town when the spell was cast escaped. Stay close."

****

Inside, the café was like the street and as cold as the inside of a walk-in freezer. Every chair and table was covered in frost, and the patrons were frozen in place. It was like a scene from a horror movie. The Widow Lowery held a teacup out as though ready to drink. The sheriff looked like he'd been laughing before the spell fixed his expression in place. Molly stood as frozen in place as the others, a tray in one hand and a plate of food in the other. Her expression was as startled as the rest in the café, and Vanessa decided everyone had known what was happening to them but all were powerless to escape.

The café was devoid of warmth, as though the heat had been sucked out of the rooms and replaced with glacial cold. A fine dusting of frost covered every surface, from floor to ceiling. Everything was chalk white. It was surreal, but the worst part was the people. They had been caught by surprise as they had gone about their daily routines. A man sat in his chair with a cup of coffee halfway up to his mouth. A couple were caught in an argument, and a child about three or four was frozen in a sprint to reach his mother's outstretched arms.

"You mentioned that someone cast a spell," Vanessa said. "Do you think it was Rammon?"

Greyeyes glanced toward Vanessa and shook his head. "This is beyond his skill. He must have had help."

She hated the idea that Rammon would have had help. That couldn't be good. "Can we undo the spell?"

He hesitated. "Some spells can't be reversed. What I do know that if the magical storm arrives before we've found a solution, no power on earth or from the sky can reverse it. The storm will make the spell permanent, and all of these people will die."

"How much time do we have?"

"Midnight tonight."

"That is also the time when I can return to my own time."

He nodded slowly. "This is not your world, Vanessa. Your life is in another time and place."

Vanessa rubbed the butterfly tattoo on her wrist. Before the cave, the tattoo had been black and white. Now the color combinations kept changing. She wished it would settle on a color. The image seemed to move under her touch like the currents of a stream. Was what Greyeyes said true, that she didn't belong here? The truth was she didn't know anymore where she belonged or why she'd been given the tattoo. She did know she couldn't stand by and do nothing.

"How much time do we have?"

"We have eight hours. Wait for me here. I need to check the back room."

He was always doing that. Leaving and telling her to stay behind. "We have to free these people." Vanessa made the comment more to herself than to Greyeyes. She couldn't shake the feeling that there was something she could do. The feeling seemed to gain momentum, circling in her thoughts—like the flight of a bird of prey as it narrowed in on its next victim. But unlike the bird of prey with its goal in mind, the solution of how to free these people evaded her.

The people looked like they were in pain. Was this just the image of their last moment before they were spelled? Or were they suffering? Did their expression indicate that they were aware of what had happened to them? She shivered at the thought. She couldn't bear it. She had to do something.

Molly resembled a mannequin in a storefront window, not flesh and blood, and it was creeping Vanessa out. Vanessa remembered two romance movies about mannequins that had come to life. She and her mother had watched them one night on television. It had been Vanessa's birthday that evening, and her mother splurged on pizza, popcorn, and chocolate swirl ice cream.

The plot line was simple. Both mannequins were cursed back in ancient times and magically turned back into human form in the present after their interaction with a human. In the first movie the mannequin turned into a human and was an artist's muse, and the second movie involved a necklace.

Her mother loved the movies because for her they were examples that anything was possible. Well, over the past few days she'd learned that magic was real but not how to tap into it herself.

To make Molly more comfortable, Vanessa took the plate of food from her and accidentally brushed her hand. The tattoo on Vanessa's wrist shimmered from midnight blue to aquamarine. A smudge of color returned to Molly's hand where Vanessa had touched her.

Her mother had often said butterflies symbolized rebirth. Could she bring the people back from the death spell they were under?

Impossible. That would be too simple. And how would she begin? She touched Molly's hand again and pale color tinged her friend's face. Vanessa hoped it was a sign that Molly was waking up.

Vanessa's tattoo glowed brighter in shades of healing green and gold.

She took Molly's hand in hers. It was still cold and felt like holding a block of ice.

Then the pain began. Cold cut through her like thousands of needle-sharp pins. She fought against the instinct to pull away. The thought that Molly might be experiencing this type of pain—that all the people in town might be in pain—kept Vanessa from releasing her hold on Molly.

Slowly, like the ticking of a clock as it nears the close of the hour, color returned in Molly's arms. Vanessa didn't let go. She reached for Molly's other hand and held them both in hers. Molly's hands warmed. More seconds ticked by. Color returned in Molly's neck, then traveled up her face until her skin glowed to life.

Molly blinked, let out a gasp, and collapsed into Vanessa's arms. The weight propelled Vanessa to the ground as she clung to Molly.

Greyeyes stood in the archway between the kitchen area and the restaurant café. His expression as stunned at Molly's transformation as Vanessa was. He rushed over to help Vanessa to her feet and Molly to a chair. "What happened?"

"I'm not sure exactly." Vanessa rubbed Molly's hands. "Molly, can you hear me? Please wake up."

Vanessa grappled with the reality of what had happened. Vanessa had touched Molly's hand, and everything changed. One minute Molly was no more lifelike than a mannequin, and the next minute life had returned.

"I think I broke the spell Molly was under."

Molly moaned as she held onto Vanessa's hand. "Aren't you a sight for sore eyes! I was having the most terrible nightmare, and my body felt like I fell on a pin cushion. I ache all over."

Vanessa squeezed Molly's hand, noting Greyeyes' troubled expression. What was he thinking? "Molly, it wasn't a dream. What do you remember?"

Molly rubbed her arms, flexing her fingers as though to keep the blood flowing.

"The day was normal. Maybe a little colder than usual, but we all agreed it was on account of the changing weather. We could feel it in our bones. We were talking about it when a woman came in wearing a glossy black dress and matching feathered hat. I remember thinking at the time that she reminded me of a raven. Not sure why. She just stood in the entrance as though waiting for something. She raised her arm, and a storm of frosted wind blew in from outside. I was thinking of shutting the door but couldn't move. My body throbbed and ached all over as though my skin had been stuck with thousands of pins and needles. I don't know how long I've been in this condition. I was numb, and my skin turned white."

"Frostbite spell," Greyeyes said to Vanessa. "The real question is how were you able to break it?"

Vanessa showed Greyeyes her wrist. "It was something my mother said about butterflies when I was young. She said they were connected to rebirth."

Greyeyes turned over her wrist to view the tattoo. "Its color is still forming. Odd."

Molly stood and pointed toward the window. "Wait. I think I saw the woman I was telling you about." Molly shook her head slowly. "She's gone now, but she was staring at us through the window. Probably just a shadow. My mistake."

Vanessa exchanged a glance with Greyeyes. Vanessa didn't have to be a mind reader to know what he was thinking. The woman who had cast the freezing spell was still here.

Chapter Twenty-Four

Storm clouds, plump with snow, blocked out the moon and stars as Merletta settled on the roof top of the Wylder Hotel and shifted from raven to human form. In her bird form, the cold had not bothered her. Now, in human form, the icy wind bit into her like an angry beast. She found the garments she'd stashed and dressed quickly. The weather had taken a dark turn as though reflecting the negative energy seeping into Wylder.

Merletta fingered the broken watch spring in her pocket that Vanessa had given her in her raven form. Merletta had received the thoughtful gift only days ago, and yet it seemed like a lifetime had passed. Yesterday anger and revenge had taken hold, and she had cast a spell that froze all the inhabitants living in Wylder. Tonight, watching Vanessa reverse her spell in the café, Merletta had had second thoughts.

Merletta had believed her quest to destroy the Thunderbird righteous, and innocents a casualty of a just cause. What if she had been wrong?

From her vantage point on the rooftop, she had a view of Wylder Street, the Mercantile, Lowery's Dress Shop, and Molly's Café. When Vanessa and Greyeyes had arrived at the café, she'd witnessed their shock and horror, and something inside her twisted. Instead of being pleased by their reaction, she'd felt a sudden and unexpected wave of regret at what she had done. So many innocents had been the victims of her wrath and revenge, and to what end? And then Vanessa had been able to reverse the frostbite spell.

Rammon had speculated that the sight of the spelled town would cause Greyeyes to flee to protect Vanessa. The plan would then be to track Greyeyes and Vanessa down and kill them before they reached the safety of the mountain caves.

Merletta sank down on the rooftop and dangled her legs over the edge, observing a pale light coming from inside the café. Rammon had miscalculated his enemy. She fingered the spring in her pocket again. Correction. Enemies.

A series of grunts, laced with swearing, warmed the chill air as Rammon rushed to join Merletta on the roof. "Why did you send for me? We should be ready down below when Greyeyes and the woman try to flee."

"I don't think they plan to leave," she said evenly, growing impatient with Rammon. How had she allowed herself to be talked into this madness?

He growled out an oath. "And you couldn't pick a better place to tell me? Why did we have to meet here? You know I hate heights."

"Pretend I forgot. Your plan isn't working, and if my instincts are correct, and they usually are, not only will your plan fail, but it will fail spectacularly. Greyeyes and Vanessa aren't leaving. They will stay and fight."

Rammon's eyes narrowed until they were dark slits. "How is that possible? Greyeyes is a protector. His instincts have always been to make sure those under his wing are safe before he engages in battle. The woman is vulnerable in Wylder. As soon as he saw the spell you cast, he should have left with her."

"Stop calling her 'the woman.' Her name is Vanessa. Do you know what it means?"

"A name is not important."

Merletta pushed to her feet. "You know that is not true, you mangy shapeshifter. A name is everything. Vanessa's name means, among other things, butterfly."

"Ooh. Terrifying."

Merletta's impatience grew. The man was a fool. "Vanessa's spirit animal is also a butterfly, the symbol of death as well as of rebirth. Her mother must have known, or at least suspected, its power. You were a fool to kill Vanessa's mother, thinking that would stop her child from seeking revenge. Vanessa can't be stopped, and Greyeyes sees that now as well. I'm sure of it. The light coming from the café indicates to me that Vanessa is using the power awakened in the cave to reverse my spell."

He pressed his lips together. "Leaving the pendant in the cave was a mistake. It didn't frighten Vanessa. It emboldened her. But all is not lost. Reversing your spell will drain Vanessa. We must attack now."

"I'm not so sure that is a good idea. It is time we accepted defeat."

"Defeat? We are on the verge of victory. The tribes of shapeshifters that share our cause are positioned by the train station and await my command. Have you forgotten what Vanessa and Greyeyes' ancestors did to ours? We must avenge their lives. That is the vow we took on the graves of our parents, and the vow they took on the graves of theirs, and so on and so on for as far back as our memories can record."

"Do you ever wonder if the killing has gone on long enough?"

"It will end," he said through clenched teeth, "either with their deaths or ours."

Chapter Twenty-Five

Time had run out.

Vanessa had the strength only to nod when Molly offered her something to eat before returning to tend to the others in the café. Vanessa had revived everyone and felt drained. She didn't know if she had the strength to do more than take a spoonful of her soup.

Across the street, in Greyeyes' watch shop, the clocks had begun their countdown to midnight. Her heart beat with the ticking sound and vibrated through her like the sound of death. When the clocks struck midnight, it would be time for her to return home.

No one would blame her if she left. Greyeyes would let her go because he loved her and believed she was safer in her own time than in his. The townspeople would say all the right things. They'd thank her for breaking Merletta's spell and reviving them and tell her that this was their fight, not hers.

She could walk away and never turn back.

She could leave the town and the friends she'd made.

She could leave Greyeyes…

An invisible weight pressed against her lungs, and she gasped for air. It was that same sensation she'd felt when she'd seen her mother murdered. There was the sense of loss, anger, grief. The sense of guilt that she had survived, while her mother had died.

She'd smothered the feelings, convinced she'd faced them because she hadn't fled Seattle and, from time to time, had checked in with the police to see if they had any leads about the hit-and-run driver. But she'd never really put down roots. She'd moved from job to job and apartment to apartment. Friends came and went as often as the seasons. She blamed her restlessness on being descended from Irish gypsies.

She knew that wasn't the reason.

If you couldn't connect to a person or place, you never risked a broken heart or having someone let you down.

But wasn't that what she was doing to the townspeople of Wylder, and to Greyeyes? She was letting them all down.

She didn't know if she could fix it, but she at least had to try.

What she did know was that there was a river of cycling hatred and revenge that raged, each side believing they were in the right. Each side justifying their actions. The end justified the means, in their thoughts.

Vanessa loathed those words as doubt crept in again on silent feet. Could she turn around generations of destructive thought? She was only one person.

In a short time, the window in the sky would open, and the star system shaped like a clock would take form in its super cluster. She didn't need Greyeyes' mother to complete the journey back to her own time. She had her mother's pendant and the tattoo that had awakened her magic. All she had to do was hold the pendant in one hand and raise her tattooed wrist to the sky when the clock star reached its zenith. Then, in a blink, she'd be back in the twenty-first century as though nothing had happened. She'd have her life back. But at what cost? She'd be leaving the only man she'd ever loved to a fate that would cause his death. The townspeople had accepted her as one of their own, and they had become her friends. How could she leave? Not when there might be a way to heal generations of pain.

In that moment she knew she would stay, regardless of the outcome to her own safety.

Vanessa looked toward the sky again. It was clear and crisp and studded with thousands of stars. One shooting star had shot like an arrow across the sky, and because arrows held strong magic and meaning to Native Americans, the sighting had caused a momentary truce as they debated its symbolism. A broken arrow meant peace. Arrows facing different directions symbolized war. But arrows also meant protection, or defense, as in the mountain cave.

A shooting star had caused a brief pause in the fighting as both sides retreated to regroup and examine the symbolism of the occurrence. Star symbolism held great significance, especially in times of war. Greyeyes stood on one end of the street with his followers, and Merletta and Rammon were at the other end with theirs. Both sides had sustained heavy casualties, and the battle had turned the white snow blood red.

If one shooting star caused a lull in the fighting, what would be the result of hundreds…thousands?

How powerful was her magic? Could she cause more stars to shoot across the sky like an arrow released from a bow? If so, would that force both sides to reexamine their reason for continuing a war that was begun centuries before any of them were born?

Molly brought a cup of tea and sat beside her. "I added a little honey to your tea. You are so pale. Can I bring you something more to eat besides soup?"

"Please don't worry about me. There are those in greater need. I am okay. Honestly." She realized that for the first time she meant those words. She had a purpose. "How is everyone?"

"Grateful and wanting to help, and for me, keeping busy keeps my mind occupied. It wanders into the most unusual places. We're all pitching in to make sure the children and those too old to fight are settled comfortably in my root cellar, and Greyeyes and Corbin are organizing the volunteers. There are many who want to help. Holt, and his father, and Abraham, and the women from the Social Club who can shoot have all joined the volunteers, with more of the townspeople on their way. But I fear it won't be enough. An army of men and wild animals have gathered by the train station, waiting for the signal to destroy Wylder."

Molly glanced toward the window, and sheer terror flashed across her eyes. She shuddered. "They aren't men or animals, are they? I heard them called shapeshifters." She resembled a deer caught in the headlights of an oncoming truck as she grew more gripped by fear. "How is such a thing possible? I've tried to keep my thoughts focused on cooking and waiting tables, but this is like a never-ending nightmare. When *will* it end?"

Vanessa shook her head slowly. "I'm the wrong person to ask, and I grew up listening to my mother's tales of banshees and headless horsemen. Until I arrived in Wylder, I thought my mother's stories were just that—stories."

Molly lowered her voice. "You have magic in you too, but your kind is the good kind. That's a type of magic I'd like to see more of."

"Me too, and thank you. I'm trying to figure it all out as I go."

Some of the fear in Molly's expression eased. "Not all shapeshifters are the bad sort. Your man has the heart and soul of a hero, and the way he looks at you gives a person a reason to believe that love exists. Well, I'd better get back to feeding the volunteers. It's going to be a hard night."

Vanessa nodded as Molly bustled around the tables, taking orders and giving hugs. Molly had called Greyeyes "that man of yours," which had caused Vanessa's heart to flutter unexpectedly at the possibility it might be true. But along with the thrill of how it made her feel was also sadness. She might lose him to Rammon's revenge.

She rose from her chair to stand beside the window. Outside, an unnatural calm had settled over the town. Calm before the storm, as they say. More like the calm before the end of the world as she knew it.

The door to the café opened on a gust of ice-cold wind as Merletta entered.

Greyeyes had been talking with volunteers in the back of the room, but when the door opened, he reached the entrance in long angry strides. "You are not welcome here," he said to Merletta. "Haven't you done enough?"

"I am here because of what I've done." Merletta glanced in the direction of Corbin and then toward Vanessa. "You must make Greyeyes listen to reason. Without my help, everyone in the town will die."

Corbin's hands were balled at his side as he approached. "What kind of trick is this?"

A tear rolled down her cheek unheeded. "Corbin, you always knew what I was and my purpose, and still there was a time when you confessed you loved me. You saw something in me then, and I'm pleading—begging—you to see it again." Her voice broke. "I was wrong."

Corbin's face was as hard as glass, but his hands relaxed as he moved toward her. The contradiction seemed to mirror what he must be feeling. "What changed your mind?"

Vanessa roped her arm through Greyeyes' and felt his tension pour into her as he spoke to Merletta. "You are asking us to trust that you have changed. We have fought each other for decades, and now you are asking us to trust you?"

"Maybe Merletta is sincere," Vanessa said. "We should at least hear her out."

Greyeyes jerked a nod and motioned for Merletta to continue.

"You are outnumbered, and Rammon intends to kill every living thing here in his quest to end you and Vanessa." Her voice caught on a sob. "The whole endless march of death has to end. For the first time I saw the madness in Rammon's eyes. The death of others means nothing to him. Life means nothing. Only revenge holds meaning. I was going down that same path. I had to stop. More than that. We must stop Rammon. He won't stop with destroying Wylder. He is aware of the century where Vanessa lives. The same century where Greyeyes' mother and sister traveled. Rammon has traveled there before and killed Vanessa's mother, and when the clock portal opens, he will travel to Vanessa's time again and kill Greyeyes' mother and sister."

"My mother and sister never intended to stay in Vanessa's city long. They didn't even tell me where they were headed, but I know they will suspect Rammon will come after them if we fail. But you said it yourself," Greyeyes said. "We are outnumbered."

Merletta heaved a sigh. "That could also work to our advantage. Rammon would never expect us to launch an attack. He knew of the magic that flowed through Vanessa's family ancestry and feared its release. It is the one power that, when combined with Greyeyes' abilities, could defeat him. Vanessa's mother knew of this power and that she was hunted because of it. That was the reason she moved from place to place." Merletta turned toward Vanessa. "Your mother used her magic to keep you hidden from Rammon so that when he killed her, he never realized she had a daughter...until you arrived in Wylder."

Vanessa held onto Greyeyes like a lifeline. She had the name of her mother's killer. She'd always suspected the hit-and-run driver had murdered her mother in cold blood, and now Merletta had confirmed her worst fears. All her life she'd imagined what she would do when she discovered the name of the person who had run her mother down.

What would she do if she had the chance to confront Rammon?

She swallowed and pushed down the thought. "I don't understand. Rammon fears I'll combine my powers with Greyeyes', and yet he still wants to fight?"

"It is because he believes you have not reached

your full potential. I made sure he knew that no one had ever reversed one of my spells. He believes if he doesn't strike now, he may never have another opportunity."

"All I've done so far was reverse your spell. My power is the healing kind rather than the aggressive, world-ending kind."

Merletta cast Vanessa a gentle smile. "And I hope your power remains as a healing force. The world needs healing, not more aggression. As your powers grow, your sight will heighten as well. But in Rammon's madness, all he sees is that magic, whatever its source, can be turned to darkness, and used for power and control. If we could lure Rammon and his shapeshifters to a place where they were surrounded and felt outnumbered or in danger of losing the battle, we might have a chance of killing him."

"Or capturing him," Vanessa said. But the words caught in her throat. Did she want him captured? A part of her wanted him dead. She fingered the butterfly pendant her mother had given her. At the time, she hadn't believed the words her mother had spoken, or understood the reasons behind the gift of a butterfly pendant. Her mother had said butterflies symbolized transformation and hope and the courage to embrace a change that would make life better. Had her mother foreseen her own death and tried to give advice?

Vanessa shook her head. "Rammon's death would make him a martyr and fuel more bloodshed. He must be captured, not killed."

Merletta gave Vanessa a slight bow. "You heal and you are wise. I understand now why Greyeyes loves you. Yes, capturing our enemy will be our goal. But we might not have a choice."

"True," Greyeyes said. "But if we could lure him and his shapeshifters away to a controlled location—or better yet, ambush him—we might have a chance."

"There is something else to consider," Corbin said. "I've started to overhear rumblings amongst the shapeshifters. Many have grown as weary as we have under the constant cloud of war. There have been numerous defectors already, and that might be one of the reasons Rammon is feeling desperate to take out Vanessa and Greyeyes. He needs a win to continue the war."

Gus, the undertaker, cleared his throat as he approached. "I couldn't help but overhear. Merletta mentioned a place where you could ambush Rammon, and I know of a location that would be perfect—the Wylder Cemetery. Reaching there without dying might be a challenge, however."

Chapter Twenty-Six

The night sky was clear and crisp, as though the moon and stars wanted an unobstructed view of the impending battle.

The plan was straightforward, with Vanessa as the bait. She would lure Rammon and his shapeshifters through town to the Wylder Cemetery on the outskirts of town. Everyone agreed that Rammon would grow suspicious if Greyeyes didn't accompany her. Greyeyes hated the plan. It put the woman he loved in jeopardy.

With Rammon watching Vanessa and Greyeyes, the townspeople would have the chance to get into position at the cemetery. To Greyeyes' relief, it hadn't taken much to get the attention of Rammon and his shapeshifters. Rammon had scouts on the café's street, and as soon as Vanessa and Greyeyes mounted their horses, word reached Rammon. It was a race to stay ahead of the shapeshifters long enough to reach the cemetery without being attacked.

Greyeyes kept a heart-stopping pace and was not surprised that Vanessa stayed with him as they raced through town on horseback. She was an extraordinary woman, with a depth of strength he'd rarely seen in someone as young. Merletta and Corbin had confirmed that all winged shapeshifters were loyal to them, but that left the four-legged predators. The coyotes were skilled and unpredictable, and the wolves dangerous.

But if Corbin's assessment proved correct, the numbers of Rammon's followers had dwindled significantly, which might give them a chance at defeating Rammon.

Greyeyes, with Vanessa at his side, sped past the center of town. He kept track of the places they passed—Wylder's Mercantile, McCabe & McClain Law Office, and the Fire House, then on to Dugan's Blacksmith Shop and St. Joseph's Episcopal Church. Each store and landmark they passed meant they were closer to their destination.

Finally, they reached the stockyards on Copper Alley, and Bone Orchard Road, which led to the cemetery only a short distance away.

A wolf jumped into their path, blocking their way. He growled low as six more shapeshifter wolves joined him.

Startled, Greyeyes' horse reared as Vanessa's, a seasoned war horse, tossed his head and pranced from side to side.

Greyeyes kept his voice calm and even as he quieted his horse with a gentle hand. "On my signal, head for the cemetery."

She shook her head. "I won't leave—"

"That was not a suggestion." He leapt from his horse and slapped Vanessa's mount on the rump. Her horse took off like a shooting star as Greyeyes charged the wolf pack.

Chapter Twenty-Seven

Heart pounding, and with only the light from the moon and stars to guide her, Vanessa raced down Bone Orchard Road toward the gates of the cemetery and heard the howl of a coyote in the distance. Greyeyes was fighting the wolves and keeping them occupied, but the coyotes must have been instructed to hunt her down. She hated that she'd had to leave Greyeyes alone to battle the wolves, but there was more than their lives at stake now. The fate of the town depended on the plan succeeding.

As Gus had mentioned, the entrance through the gate was narrow, only wide enough to allow a few people to walk abreast or let a small wagon through at one time. Which was perfect for their plan. The narrow passageway forced the shapeshifters to form a line rather than advance in a group. The first part of the plan was that the townspeople would have arrived at the cemetery before Vanessa and hidden in the shadows. When the coyotes arrived, the volunteers would pick them off one by one as they funneled through the gate's entrance.

A good plan on paper, but it relied on a lot of things working perfectly.

Under the glow of the full moon, she kept a steady pace as she guided her horse past gravesite markers. Some of the graves were marked with a simple cross, while others had elaborate markers made from stone. According to Gus, the grave marker she was searching for was better described as a mausoleum and was one of the largest in the cemetery.

It had been built by a wealthy rancher for his only daughter, who died on the eve of her wedding. The mausoleum was a replica of one he'd seen in the Green-Wood Cemetery in New York, commemorating the loss of a daughter who had died at the age of seventeen and also on the eve of her wedding.

The mausoleum was seventeen feet tall and seventeen feet wide, with seventeen roses etched into the stone. Unlike the one at the New York cemetery, the rancher in Wylder had added an underground catacomb with a secret entrance where he and his wife could visit his daughter's grave in private.

And then, as she rounded a corner, twin lights flickered in the breeze. The mausoleum stood on a knoll in the middle of the cemetery, and as promised, Gus had lit the torches on either side of the entrance…a beacon of light and hope in an otherwise gloomy place.

She jumped off her horse and ran toward the largest mausoleum. The plan was to lure Rammon and his shapeshifters into that tomb.

A wolf's howl tore at the sky as he paused at the cemetery gates briefly. She shivered, and her blood ran cold. She couldn't tell if the wolf's howl was one of victory over defeating Greyeyes, or defeat that the man she loved had escaped.

She clung to the hope that Greyeyes had escaped as she ran.

From the corner of her eye, she saw Corbin, Holt, and men from Holt's horse ranch, as well as the sheriff's deputies, signal her from the protection of the shadows. She nodded and kept running. The howls of both wolves and coyotes followed her. She stole a glance over her shoulder. The coyote shapeshifters had joined the wolves and had taken off in her direction.

At the steps of the mausoleum, she grabbed one of the lighted torches on the wall beside the entrance and pushed open the unlocked stone door. The entrance gaped open like an ominous black hole. She didn't hesitate as she leapt over the threshold.

She descended the stairs two at a time. The chamber at the bottom was larger than the outside dimensions of the building would suggest. A lone casket lay in the center of a marble floor. The loneliness of the simple casket struck her as sad. She would have expected the caskets of the parents to have been buried beside their daughter. Had they moved away, perhaps? Another mystery in a town that had as many as the stars in the skies.

She headed toward the south-facing wall where she had been told the constellation of Orion had been etched into the stone. A low growl drew her attention to the top of the stairs. The shapeshifters were already entering the mausoleum.

Although she still held the torch, its light cast only a small circle around her. Merletta had described how Vanessa's vision would change as well as how to identify the shapeshifters, especially Rammon. Because of her heightened sight, she was able to see what she could only describe as the thermal images of the shapeshifters. Or maybe it was more like their auras. Whatever it was, she knew in an instant that Rammon was not among the shapeshifters who had followed her to the mausoleum. His aura had a distinct, iridescent, dark purple hue, like molten lava as it made its way down the mountain to the sea.

At the top of the stairs, dozens of glowing eyes stared at her in the dark. The shapeshifters growled low as they crept toward her, predators seeking their prey. Her fear grew with every step they took. The instinct to flee was strong.

"Not yet," she whispered. "Not yet."

Then, when the last shapeshifter had crossed the entrance into the mausoleum, the door slammed shut on a gust of frozen wind. Ice spread and crackled over its surface, sealing it shut in a solid sheet of ice.

Merletta had kept her promise and cast her spell, and with it had sealed the fate of everyone locked inside the mausoleum.

Silence echoed through the stone tomb as reality seized the shapeshifters. They were trapped. A collective roar of rage, laced with panic, swept over the shapeshifters as they realized they'd been tricked.

If the next step didn't work, she'd be trapped here as well. But her fear was laced with an odd sense of accomplishment. As long as the shapeshifters were trapped down here with her, the town was safe. She scanned the remaining shapeshifters. The only loose end was to find Rammon.

A few of the shapeshifters raced back up the stairs, but their attempt to break down the door was futile. Others shifted into their human form, while those remaining edged toward her.

Chapter Twenty-Eight

Vanessa could almost taste the fear, panic, and rage in the air as the shapeshifters realized they were trapped. She also knew that she would be their first target, and after that they would turn on each other. If she was going to escape, it had to be now.

She threw the torch in the direction of the nearest shapeshifter. The fur on his shoulder caught fire, and he yelped in pain, jumped away from the fallen torch, and shifted in order to pound out the flames.

Seizing the distraction, she pressed the North Star on the Orion constellation wall. Gears whirled and clicked behind the stones as a latch released and the outline of a door appeared. It opened inward in an escape of stale air.

She slid through the narrow space, and once she was on the other side, she shoved it closed and was immediately plunged into darkness so profound it seemed as though she had been blindfolded.

Angry voices and howls echoed behind the door when they realized she'd escaped. They beat against the door, and then she heard muffled scratching sounds and voices as they tried to duplicate how she'd opened the door. They weren't just animals, they were human, and it would be only a matter of time before they figured out how the door opened, which meant she hadn't much time to reach the surface.

The details of what to do once she'd escaped into the mausoleum's secret passage had not been clear. Gus had never used it himself. He'd only heard the stories, the rumors. Adrenaline poured through her, threatening a panic attack. What if the stories Gus had heard had been exaggerated over time? This passageway could lead to a dead end or go in circles that led her back to where she began.

She had expected her eyes to adjust to the light, but it was as dark as it was when she'd first entered. She reached out for the walls to help guide her. They were damp, cold, and slimy. She shuddered and pulled back, only to force herself to touch them again. She had to get her bearings and get as far away from the wall to the mausoleum as she could. The only way was to feel her way, because evidently this new vision power she had was limited. It must need some source of light, however small, to work.

She pushed forward for what she calculated was a matter of feet. The midnight blackness turned to a charcoal gray. A few feet more and it lightened again to the color of steel. Had her eyes adjusted, or was there a source of light?

She quickened her step.

A welcome shaft of light poured down from above.

Merletta appeared and rushed toward her, with Corbin and his men at her side. "Oh, good," Merletta said. "You're not dead. The next step is to see if the shapeshifters are reasonable. We'll give them a choice. Negotiate or be sealed into the mausoleum with a wall of ice. The staircase that leads outside is only a few feet away."

"Wait," Vanessa said, as Merletta and the men

175

turned to leave. "Have you captured Rammon?"

"He wasn't with the others?" Merletta shook her head. "You must find him before he turns others to his will."

Before Vanessa could respond, Merletta and the men vanished into the darkness of the tunnel.

Finding the stairs, she climbed, and with each step her unease and frustration grew. How was she going to find Rammon? And if she did, how could she stop him? Her powers enabled her to see a person's aura or UV image, and that extended to plants and animals as well. A cool power, but hardly the scary or useful kind when dealing with a psycho-killer like Rammon. She reached the top step and climbed to the surface under a star-dusted sky.

The cemetery was in the distance to her left, and a vast snow-dusted pastureland lay to her right, stretching to the horizon. In the distance she saw fluorescent lights moving toward her. A lone deer, perhaps? Then the light on the animal changed, or rather, became clearer, and she knew.

It was Rammon, and he was heading straight toward her at an inhuman speed.

She was out in the open. Unprotected and alone. Her only choices were to jump back into the passageway, where she'd be trapped, or to run.

Vanessa heard her mother's words in her thoughts...

You are never alone. Summon the light.

Until now, she'd never known what that meant.

There was a third choice.

Stand her ground and face the man who'd killed her mother, who had run her down with his car and murdered her like she meant nothing, like her life meant nothing.

Vanessa faced her mother's murderer.

She drew herself to her full height, spread her arms wide, and drew down the light from the stars and moon. It warmed and flowed through her. In every corner of her being. Grew. Expanded.

She sensed the moment Rammon would lunge toward her, and she pushed out her arms and willed the light and power within her to drive him back.

The force of the light lifted him into the air. He tumbled over and over and landed on the perimeter of the cemetery. He seemed dazed and surprised, but when he shook free of his confusion, he narrowed his eyes.

"You'll regret this," he shouted, his voice carrying toward her like the roll of thunder.

His shift from man to beast took less time than drawing a deep breath.

Rammon stood before her, three times the size of the shapeshifters he ruled with fear. He dropped to all fours and sped toward her, the gleam of death shining in his eyes like a promise.

For a split second she was locked in his gaze. Was this how prey felt when attacked by a predator? Aware of their fate but too afraid to flee?

Well, she might be afraid, but she would not run. She spread her arms again to summon the light. This time her muscles trembled with the strain and the light that had freely come to her aid. Had she depleted her power? Was her gift the kind that needed time to rebuild?

Questions spun unanswered as Rammon drew closer and closer.

He was less than a heartbeat away.

She held out her arms, gritted her teeth and prayed.

But as Rammon leapt into the air to attack, Greyeyes let out a war cry, jumped from his galloping horse, and drove Rammon to the ground, then balled up his fist and knocked the shapeshifter unconscious.

"You're alive!" She hadn't known the depths of her fears, her love, until he stood before her. Bloodied, clothes torn to shreds, but alive. He was the most wonderful sight she'd ever seen. She leapt into his arms. "Don't leave me like that again. When we fight...we fight together."

He chuckled and nodded. "I saw what you did. There's power in you. No wonder Rammon was afraid."

"He didn't look afraid. He would have killed me if you hadn't arrived when you did."

Greyeyes wrapped his arms around her waist and pulled her against him. "I'm not so sure. I think you would have found the strength to defeat him."

With crystal clarity, she saw the love in his eyes. "But you didn't want to take the chance he might hurt me."

"You are right, my love. I didn't want to take the chance. Your powers will continue to build over time, and what a glorious power they will be."

She lifted her chin and studied the play of shadows over his chiseled face. She saw strength as well as a deep well of love reflected in his gaze. In a short span of time, this man had become as important to her as the air she breathed, and he'd called her "his love."

"You love me."

"How could I not?"

"I love you too."

"And I am blessed because of it." He glanced toward the night sky. "You missed your window to return home. But perhaps there is another path."

She placed her fingers over his lips to still his words. "I would ask for a kiss to seal our bond. I am exactly where I want to be. You, my valiant warrior, are my home."

"And you, my fearless and brave heart of my heart, are my world." He brushed his lips against hers and deepened the kiss.

A word about the author...

Pam Binder is an award-winning Amazon, *New York Times*, and *USA Today* Bestselling author. Pam writes young adult, romance, historical, time travel, and fantasy fiction. *Publishers Weekly* has said: "Binder gracefully weaves elements of humor, magic and romantic tensions into her novels."

Pam's favorite place on earth is Ireland, and her favorite pastime is sharing adventures with her husband, children, and grandchildren.

Thank you for purchasing
this publication of The Wild Rose Press, Inc.

For questions or more information
contact us at
info@thewildrosepress.com.

The Wild Rose Press, Inc.

CPSIA information can be obtained
at www.ICGtesting.com
Printed in the USA
LVHW041333230822
726646LV00008B/309